"You're . . . pushing me into the mood to stomp a ditch in your big, stupid ass . . ." said Longarm.

A good six inches shorter than Longarm, the quarrelsome drunk growled, "That a fuckin' fact, little man?" The booze-saturated bully telegraphed his first ham-fisted blow.

In a blur of controlled, concentrated action, Longarm's right hand snaked to the ivory grips of his Colt .45. The heavy steel barrel slammed against Duer's rock-hard noggin. The sickening crack of metal against bone opened a long, ugly gash on Duer's face.

. . . Amarillo's most famous ass kicker went down like a pole-axed steer. Longarm's clenched left fist came around and caught the man with a thunderous, devastating lick flush against the jaw. Duer's head snapped sideways toward the bar.

Duer coughed, crawled several feet, gagged, then spit a strangling gob of blood and teeth. Somehow, he grabbed a table leg, pulled up onto his knees, and almost got himself into a standing position again.

One gambler, who'd backed into a corner, said, "Jesus, why don't he stay down? The feller that's kickin' his big, dumb ass don't appear to be the least bit tired."

TABOR EVANS

LONGARM

AND THE
PALO DURO MONSTER

JOVE BOOKS, NEW YORK

THE BERKLEY PUBLISHING GROUP
Published by the Penguin Group
Penguin Group (USA) Inc.
375 Hudson Street, New York, New York 10014, USA
Penguin Group (Canada), 90 Eglinton Avenue East, Suite 700, Toronto, Ontario M4P 2Y3, Canada
(a division of Pearson Penguin Canada Inc.)
Penguin Books Ltd., 80 Strand, London WC2R 0RL, England
Penguin Group Ireland, 25 St. Stephen's Green, Dublin 2, Ireland (a division of Penguin Books Ltd.)
Penguin Group (Australia), 250 Camberwell Road, Camberwell, Victoria 3124, Australia
(a division of Pearson Australia Group Pty. Ltd.)
Penguin Books India Pvt. Ltd., 11 Community Centre, Panchsheel Park, New Delhi—110 017, India
Penguin Group (NZ), 67 Apollo Drive, Rosedale, North Shore 0632, New Zealand
(a division of Pearson New Zealand Ltd.)
Penguin Books (South Africa) (Pty.) Ltd., 24 Sturdee Avenue, Rosebank, Johannesburg 2196,
South Africa

Penguin Books Ltd., Registered Offices: 80 Strand, London WC2R 0RL, England

This is a work of fiction. Names, characters, places, and incidents either are the product of the author's imagination or are used fictitiously, and any resemblance to actual persons, living or dead, business establishments, events, or locales is entirely coincidental.

LONGARM AND THE PALO DURO MONSTER

A Jove Book / published by arrangement with the author

PRINTING HISTORY
Jove edition / February 2009

ISBN: 978-0-515-14585-4

JOVE®
Jove Books are published by The Berkley Publishing Group,
a division of Penguin Group (USA) Inc.,
375 Hudson Street, New York, New York 10014.
JOVE® is a registered trademark of Penguin Group (USA) Inc.
The "J" design is a trademark of Penguin Group (USA) Inc.

PRINTED IN THE UNITED STATES OF AMERICA

10   9   8   7   6   5   4   3   2   1

Chapter 1

Deputy U.S. Marshal Custis Long—known far and wide to all and sundry as the iron-fisted long arm of federal law enforcement—leaned back in his chair. A satisfied, nigh on beatific smile played across his ruggedly handsome face. Ensconced in a favorite thronelike seat, at a preferred corner table in Denver's Holy Moses Saloon, he twirled the ends of his droopy moustache, then ran a finger back and forth beneath it along his curled upper lip.

A quick glance at his freshly emptied plate atop the immaculate, cloth-covered table confirmed that he'd finished every bite of a damned fine piece of perfectly singed beefsteak and all the trimmings. Polished off four glasses of ice-cold beer. At that singular moment in time the stalwart lawman figured as how he was about as satisfied with the world as a man in his kind of potentially deadly profession could legitimately expect. Yes, indeed, life was damned good—especially during those relaxed periods when some black-hearted skunk wasn't firing blue whistlers his direction.

With a leisurely flourish, he fished a nickel cheroot from the vest pocket of his brown tweed suit. Fired the fresh stogie—hand-rolled on the sweaty, glistening thighs of beautiful Cuban women—with a sulfur match scratched to blazing life on the butt of the ivory-gripped Colt Frontier model pistol lying across his full belly. A roiling, bluish gray cloud of aromatic tobacco smoke soon circled above his head like a growing cyclone.

As the smoldering match dropped from his fingers into the spittoon next to his chair, he cast a lecherous glance across the room. My, oh my, he thought, as he watched the eye-catching Cora Anne Fisher strut her high-breasted, narrow-waisted, black-haired, ruby-lipped self from one table of the saloon's combination bar and restaurant to the next.

The stunning woman placed a friendly hand on the shoulder of and leaned close to each grinning male patron she visited. The dip of her low-cut gown gifted the leering goober with a fine view of her ample bosom. She spoke several words of welcome, smiled, patted the leering man on the shoulder, then moved on to the next gent.

Without fail, she also managed to cast a knowing wink Longarm's direction. Occasionally, she would turn, strike a pose so no one else could see, and stealthily caress herself in the most fetching way for his, and only his, benefit. Hers was a secret, sensual display designed to let Longarm know exactly what was in store as soon as they had settled in her private rooms once again.

Long inhaled a deep, pleasing lung of the heavy smoke, rolled the cigar from one side of his mouth to the other with his tongue, then winked back at his stunning paramour. Under his breath and to no one in particular, he muttered, "God, but I do love this joint. Be fine as frog's hair with me if I could just move in here and live."

The voluptuous and ever-willing Cora Fisher was only a part of why Longarm liked the Holy Moses Saloon so

2

much—a very large part but still and all only a part. He reveled in the comfortable, pleasant, peaceful atmosphere. Found homelike solace in everything from the dark paneled walls, heavy glass windows, well-stocked bar, and shining, mirrored back bar.

The fact that no noisy gambling devices like a roulette wheel, faro table, goose-and-balls, or craps table were in evidence suited him right down to the polished hardwood floor. Additionally, no tinkling piano, twanging banjo, or other distracting, tinny music jangled the nerves of those regular patrons who sought the tranquillity of a serene place to drink and a relaxing spot to discuss the events of the day.

As proprietor and working manager of the Holy Moses, Cora Fisher permitted poker games, but only if assured any extraneous noise would be kept to an absolute minimum. The good food, fine liquors, closeness of the space, peace and quiet, and attentiveness of Mike O'Hara—the saloon's gregarious bartender—all went into the mix of Longarm's continuously growing affection for Denver's newest and most agreeable watering hole. When his ass wasn't being pounded to powder by a hammer-headed cayuse out on the trail, the weary lawdog couldn't wait to get to Cora's wondrous joint and relax.

Near as Longarm could tell, Cora had fashioned her Rocky Mountain oasis in the pattern of an East Coast private club for men. A haven of calm and solitude in a bustling, noisy city. Expressly designed for the patronage of discerning gents gifted with discriminating tastes and wallets large enough to maintain their continued return. Longarm could not have been more pleased with the overall result of her efforts.

After visiting every occupied table in the room, Cora sashayed to Longarm's corner spot of tranquil refuge, then eased her shapely caboose into the chair nearest the relaxed, virtually satiated lawdog. Out of sight, her inquisitive hand's energetic fingers tickled their way up to the juncture of his legs. The talented digits found what they sought, wrapped around it, then gently squeezed.

Aroused by Cora's bolder-than-brass advances, Custis Long rose, ever so slightly, in his seat. His thick dark eyebrows knitted and his breathing sharpened. He barely heard the woman when she hissed, "You just think we raised the roof last night, Custis. Wait till I get you back upstairs after closing tonight."

Of a sudden, the previous evening's carnal dance flashed across the backs of the ever-ready deputy marshal's eyelids—almost like a lantern show he'd once witnessed in a traveling carnival. Cora had been out running errands when he'd first arrived at her fancy cantina earlier the day before. But she'd spotted him, sipping on a glass of Maryland rye at his favored table, within seconds of her return.

Nearly two months of separation, brought on by Longarm's pursuit of a brutal killer named Wolf Magruder across most of New Mexico Territory's Jornada del Muerto, had honed the striking Cora's sexual hunger to a keenly stropped razor's edge. She'd charged across the near empty barroom like a Texas tornado, grabbed the more-than-willing lawman's hand, and dragged him up the back staircase to her private quarters.

Weapons, boots, shoes, and clothing of every sort flew in all directions. Their accoutrement landed in odd places around the room as though caught up in the destruction of a sexual whirlwind. Within a matter of what seemed like seconds, the pair were stark naked, locked in a gasping, grasping, sucking, hedonistic embrace and stumbling toward the panting woman's monstrous bed. Longarm's hands dropped to Cora Fisher's finely shaped buttocks and lifted her off

4

the floor. She climbed his sinewy, muscled body like a line stringer for that new contraption called the telephone, then encircled his waist with muscular, milky white thighs.

One of Cora's hands gripped his neck as the other darted down between the grunting couple and guided her energetic lover's enormous dong to the threshold of her dripping muff. When convinced he was positioned in just the right spot, she abruptly shoved her ass downward with as much force as she could muster, given her position.

An immediate gush and fluttering of an amazingly active, steamy cooze around his throbbing tool caused Longarm to throw his head back and groan with pleasure. With every ounce of arm strength he could bring to bear on the problem, Longarm tightened his grip on Cora's behind, bounced the woman up and down on the iron-hard rod of muscle between his legs, and unerringly stumbled for the bed. Three more steps, and they'd finally made it.

With a mighty push from powerfully built legs, he launched the duo onto the thick, waiting mattress. Anvil-solid, pile-driving buttocks drilled his turgid prong into Cora's willing flesh with the speed of a steam-powered pushrod on a Baldwin locomotive.

Squeaks and squeals of pure, wanton, joyful pleasure shamelessly popped from between the flushed, sweat-covered Cora's bloodred lips. With one hand she caressed a melon-sized, sheen-covered breast and pinched a nipple already erect with carnal excitement. The other hand crept down her slick belly, until an extended middle finger found the budlike bulge in the cleft amidst the thatch-covered juncture between her flailing legs.

As Longarm watched the wanton show Cora had going for him, his near frantic lover vigorously rubbed the blood-distended flesh beneath her talented fingers. From behind heavy-lidded eyes, she further inflamed him by whispering, "Oh, oh, oh, yes. Oh, yes. That's it. Deeper. All of it. Jam it all in. Harder. Do it harder, baby. Oh God, oh God, oh God."

The hand left her breast and grabbed his neck again. She pulled herself up, licked his ear, sucked the lobe, then hissed, "God, you're good. Make me pop so hard it splatters all over both of us."

Longarm worked at the project Cora had gasped into his ear like a man possessed. After what seemed like nearly an hour of muscle-knotting effort with the girl on her back, he rolled her onto her stomach, jerked her up onto trembling knees, and went at the body-sapping assignment from a different direction. Her yelping immediately got more intense as the knobbed head of his throbbing dong rubbed new, more intensely sensitive spots deep inside her gushing nook.

He felt things were going pretty well, when, to his eternal surprise, she jerked loose, twirled around, and pushed him onto his back. Facing him, she swung a leg over his hips, slid her sloppy, sopping bush down the shaft of his rigid tool, and rode him like a bronco-busting Texas brush popper on a never-before-been-broken hay burner. The ride continued for so long, he began to think she'd never get off. After a while, Longarm crossed his arms behind his head and simply laid there, enjoying the wondrous, bouncing boob show going on a few inches above his mouth.

Then, of a sudden, the scenario changed again. With eyes glazed over like she'd spent hours in an opium den, Cora rolled out of the bed, flopped onto the thick, plush, Turkish carpet on the floor below, raised her legs, and beckoned for him to come on down. The shameless couple did the horizontal two-step there on the floor, then moved to a love seat that almost collapsed from their energetic abuse. They banged the hell out of each other while standing against the door that led to the stairway. Cora yelped and whinnied so much Longarm worried that patrons of the saloon below must surely hear them.

And just when he thought the entire show had all but run its course and he was on the verge of dropping a load that would easily fill a leather pounder's ten-gallon hat, there was a barely discernable knock at the back entrance of his insatiable mate's apartment. Longarm knew the door led to a private, closed, exterior staircase. Those hidden steps dropped along the side of the building and thence into a narrow alleyway between the Holy Moses and a busy Chinese laundry.

Drenched in sweat, he had Cora's legs wrapped his neck when he stopped humping long enough to gasp, "You expectin' someone, darlin'?"

An impish grin flashed across her lips, then just as quickly disappeared. She pushed a breast up, licked the nipple, then said, "Maybe."

"Who?"

His rail-stiff pecker slapped against a rock-hard belly as Cora pulled loose and scampered away from the lustful action. Still buck-assed naked, drenched in the froth of sex, and smelling exactly like what they'd been doing, she padded across the room barefoot. She glanced through the entry's hidden peephole, then quickly unlocked the door and snatched it open.

Longarm, perched on the edge of the bed like a large featherless bird, watched the unfolding goings-on at the door and occasionally stroked his still inflexible rod. Cora spoke to someone he couldn't see, then moved aside. A petite, blond-haired beauty draped in a floor-length, dove gray capelike affair stepped across the threshold, then pushed the entry shut behind her. The door made a muted click as it closed, then Cora snapped the dead bolts into place.

Hand in hand, like a pair of mischievous school girls about to do something they'd been warned against in numerous Baptist Sunday school lessons, the women strode toward him, then stopped a few feet away from his spot on the bed. The visitor's gaze locked onto the flush-faced lawman's rampant joy handle.

Her aquamarine-colored eyes widened as she sucked in a deep, sharp breath. The back of one hand went to trembling lips. "Sweet Jesus, Cora," she gasped, "there's a lot more to 'im than you let on. Not sure I've ever even seen one that big before." Then, as if to herself she added, "Always wanted to, though."

Cora Fisher flashed a wicked, lusty grin as she moved to a spot slightly behind the blue-eyed beauty, then reached over and pulled at the tie string on the girl's cape. The heavy cloak dropped to the floor and bunched up in a lumpy heap at their bare feet.

The stunning visitor was totally naked. A head shorter than Cora, the girl was nonetheless gifted with a near flawless figure. Firm, melon-sized breasts sported dark areolas tipped with erect, blood-engorged nipples as big as a grown man's thumb. Her narrow waist flared into ample hips. The entire package was highlighted by a triangle of downy blond pubic hair that looked like corn silk growing in a fist-sized patch at the juncture of her shapely legs.

Longarm's dingus rang like a brass dinner bell when Cora ran a hand up the blonde's side, caressed one of the unflinching stranger's generous boobs, then tweaked the erect, stiffening nipple.

The mysterious girl moaned and leaned against Cora. She closed already heavy-lidded eyes, laid her head on Cora's

8

shoulder, then reached back and slid a hand up between the taller woman's already spread legs.

Amid quickened breaths and gasps of pleasure, Cora hissed, "Remember me telling you . . . I knew another woman . . . who wanted to spend the night with us?"

Somehow, Longarm felt that whole sections of his brain had suddenly emptied of anything like reasonable thought. A chaotic mind seemed to have gone totally blank. His lust-heated gaze darted back and forth between the naked, writhing bodies but a few feet away. The pair's mutual caressing became more urgent.

"Uh-h-h, yeah. Think I remember something like that," he grunted.

Unable to take his attention off the women's wickedly involved actions, he watched as the shapely blonde twisted ever so slightly and licked Cora's neck. The owner of the Holy Moses closed her eyes, and her head lolled to one side, then she said, "This is Minnie Clay, Custis. Come on over here and introduce her to that wonderful thing between your legs."

Longarm stood. He boldly stepped up so close to the exquisitely shaped Minnie Clay that the tip of his rod rubbed against the girl's table-flat belly.

Minnie's hand snaked out and closed around the steely saber of love between them. "Sweet merciful Father," she gasped as tremulous fingers slid up and down the shaft of the mammoth sword of veined flesh. "It's even bigger close up." She shot a wink up at Longarm, then quipped, "Wouldn't want to get hit in the head with this thing."

In a flash, Minnie pulled away from Cora's insistent fingers and mouth, grasped Longarm's love muscle more urgently, and led him back to the rumpled bed. She flopped onto the scrambled mess of sheets and covers he and Cora had created and brought her legs up. Then, in an amazing

9

display of rubbery suppleness, spread those near perfect limbs so far apart her knees rested on the bedclothes next to her ears.

"Come on, honey," the panting girl growled. "Gimme some of that big ole thing. Aw, jeeze, gimme all of it!"

Longarm hopped up between the smoldering Minnie's legs and shoved himself into her silken, juicy, waiting glory hole. He immediately noted that, for a woman of her diminutive size, she had an amazingly roomy snatch, which she used with astonishing skill and ferocity.

For nigh on a minute, Cora Fisher just stood next to the bed, stroked her own breasts, and watched wide-eyed and open-mouthed while her well-hung lover sluiced in and out of Minnie Clay's spurting gash. Eventually, though, she just couldn't stay out of the action any longer. She licked her crimson lips, jumped into the bed, then stretched out beside the rutting couple.

One of Minnie's hands immediately dove between Cora's scissoring legs. The gasping blond beauty expertly found Cora's most sensitive spot and massaged her willing friend into a fit of breathless orgasm.

Twisting onto one side, Cora laid a tongue-filled, open-mouthed kiss on the grunting girl who bounced beneath Custis Long and, at the same time, went back to pulling, pinching, and tweaking the elfin blonde's waiting nipples. Soon, though, she slipped a bit farther down in the bed and replaced her fingers with a wet, hot mouth that made loud smacking sounds. With greedy lips, she sucked away at the heaving Minnie's super-hardened nipples.

From that point, the action became more frenzied and complex as the riotous night wore on. Every possible combination of bodies, mouths, and tongues that three people could bring to mind was tried. The women couldn't seem to get enough of Longarm, or each other. And when the ac-

10

tion appeared too slow for either girl, they had no qualms about diddling themselves in what appeared a little needed effort to keep their juices flowing.

Minnie Clay proved unendingly tireless and creative in her vigorous ability to come up with fresh approaches to mankind's oldest and most common experience. She appeared especially inspired when applying a talented tongue to the slick, wet interior of Cora's inflamed crotch, or the bulbous tip of Longarm's blood-engorged root. The gal seemed to revel in doing both at the same time.

Last thing the exhausted lawman remembered before he dropped into a sated, untroubled sleep—at about three in the morning—was watching in awed fascination as the women, end to end, went at each other like a pair of sex-starved cats.

According to his genuine, two-dollar Ingersoll railroad watch, Longarm had awakened a few minutes before noon. A tray of hot food waited on the table beside the bed. Both of his gleefully decadent lady friends were gone, but the heavy, pungent bouquet of their sex still hung in the air and clung to his body. The aroma of their musk caused an immediate boner that rose from between his legs and rang like a cathedral bell every time anything touched it.

Now, several hours later, he lounged at his favorite Holy Moses table, with Cora Fisher's insistent hand buried in his crotch again—her unrelenting fingers caressing his throbbing dong. He tried, but couldn't imagine what the relentlessly horny woman had in mind as an encore to follow up the previous night's overwhelmingly sensual three-way performance. As Cora clawed at his crotch, he wondered, then hoped, that the lovely, talented, and tireless Minnie Clay would make another spirited, inspired appearance.

About the time he turned in Cora's direction, to ask for a clarification of her somewhat cryptic statement of what might await in their immediate sexual future, a filthy-faced

11

waif who appeared not to have had a bath in at least a year strode up to their table. The grit-covered rogue snatched off his ratty snap-brimmed woolen cap, then said, "Bartender over yonder says as how you're Deputy Marshal Custis Long. Hope you're him, 'cause I ain't goin' no farther to look for the hard-to-find son of a bitch if'n you ain't."

Longarm winked at Cora, then ran a quick, evaluating look from the top of the filthy youngster's shock of greasy hair to his run-down pair of lace-poor, brogan shoes. "Yeah, I'm Long. What's it to you, bud?"

The grimy-faced urchin, who from all outward appearances had been mining coal in the Rocky Mountains for years, snatched a slip of folded paper from the pocket of his tattered jacket. He held the note up as though it was something valuable, then said, "Feller over at the Federal Courthouse gimme this here message to deliver. Said as how I should find yuh and give it to yuh."

Longarm shot a concerned-looking Cora Anne Fisher a fleeting glance, then reached in the kid's direction. The grubby scamp pulled the mysterious missive away, then said, "Same feller said as how you 'uz a rich 'un. Said as how you'd gimme a damned nice tip fer bringin' this here note to yuh."

A twisted grin etched its way across Custis Long's lips. "That a fact? And what would you consider a 'damned nice tip,' your lordship?"

Kid flashed an amazing set of nearly perfect pearly choppers and cocked his head to one side as though damned proud of himself. "Oughta be worth at least a dollar, maybe two. Gotta admit, it's a helluva hike all the way over here from Cherokee and Colfax. Think I wore nigh on an inch of leather off'n the soles of my shoes tryin' to find you, Marshal Long."

Longarm slapped his knee and chuckled. "Hell, boy,

you don't have an inch of shoe leather left on those clod-hoppers to wear off. Given you've got no laces or socks, it's a wonder to me you can even keep them big kickers on your feet."

The nervy stray didn't miss a beat when he countered with, "While that might be true, you'll have to admit, I did bring the note as instructed. Cain't believe a gentleman of your obvious breeding, upstanding character, worldliness, and fine reputation would stiff a homeless, hungry orphan whose parents was kilt by bloodthirsty injuns several years ago."

Longarm shot another corner-of-the-eye look toward Cora. He watched in bemused amazement when she flipped a five-dollar gold piece onto the table, then said, "Give the man his note, scamp. Take the money. Go get yourself a bath and some clean clothes. Then get yourself back here no later than seven tomorrow morning. Any kid who can lay out a line of horse manure like yours deserves a job, and I'm just the woman who can find plenty for you to do."

The kid snatched the money off the table quicker than a hungry chicken could peck corn out of a pie tin. Then he examined it as though sure the coin was bogus. An actual tear formed in the corner of the filthy rascal's eye when he realized the money was genuine. "Job? You ain't kiddin' now, are you? Gonna give me an actual job, lady?"

Cora made a shooing motion with one hand. "Yes, yes, and yes. Now hand Marshal Long his note, and go get cleaned up. You smell like the insides of a week dead buffalo. And, for God's sake, be sure and buy a new pair of shoes."

The grinning rogue handed over the creased sheet of paper. He slapped his shabby cap back on, did several abbreviated bows, almost danced a jig, then said, "Name's Toby Bounds. Promise you won't be sorry for the good turn you

13

done me. Be here seven o'clock sharp, missus. Promise I'll be clean, too."

Cora flicked her hand at the boy again. "Well, get on with you, Toby. I'll look for you tomorrow. And don't call me missus. You can call me Cora or Cora Anne or even Miss Fisher. But don't call me missus. Makes me sound like I'm as big as a skinned moose and have been standing in front of an iron stove all day long bakin' biscuits for my man with a squalling baby on my hip. Sweet Jesus."

A second later, the adolescent tramp was nothing more than a particularly disagreeable aroma clinging to the hairs in Longarm's nose. His initial suspicions were confirmed when he unfolded the note and found the simple message:

Custis,

Need you immediately. Don't fuck around. Come now. Billy.

P.S. Did I mention that you shouldn't fuck around!

Longarm patted Cora's hand and said, "Well, you can't begin to know how much I hate to say this, darlin'. But whatever you had in mind for tonight's dance is gonna have to wait. Appears as how, once again, Marshal Billy Vail has other plans for yours truly."

Cora flashed a wicked grin, squeezed his rising prong one more time, then said, "Well, that's unfortunate. I suppose that the best thing that's ever happened to you, or to any man for that matter, will just have to wait till you can get back from your newest adventure. Won't it?"

Longarm cast a woeful glance at the scrap of paper between his fingers. He shot another at the grinning Cora Fisher just in time to watch the tip of her tongue run from one side of her ruby-lipped mouth to the other. Then the fingers wrapped around his prong applied just the right amount of pressure. A barely audible groan escaped his twitching lips.

"Yeah," the squirming lawdog gasped. "Guess we'll just have to wait—damn it all."

Chapter 2

Marshal Billy Vail's edgy, bespectacled chief clerk jumped as though shot when Longarm slammed his way into their boss's outer office. Startled and surprised by the deputy's bearish, abrupt entrance, the owl-eyed Henry hopped away from a job at his newfangled typewriting apparatus. He came nigh on to standing at attention, coughed, and with a visible display of teeth-gritting irritation waved his private kingdom's most recent invader toward the open door of the U.S. marshal's inner sanctum. Grumbled indecipherable epithets issued from the fussy gent's twisted mouth as he flounced into his seat and went back to hunting-and-pecking at the ivory-colored keys of the clattering iron machine perched atop his desk like a hungry black buzzard.

Longarm strode through the open office door and up to Vail's desk. He tapped on one corner of the massive piece of mahogany furniture with a nervous finger. Then, with no invitation proffered, flopped into his boss's overstuffed, tack-decorated, Moroccan leather guest chair. He dropped his snuff brown Stetson on the floor beside the seat and did a quick study of Billy Vail's haggard, moonlike face.

Vail appeared troubled and did not speak for almost a

minute. During that passage of time, Longarm's much-imposed-on boss was consumed by the text of a telegraph message he held in one trembling hand. Eventually Vail tossed the page aside and pushed back into his own chair. Several more seconds of silence passed before he finally grunted, ran a hand from forehead to chin, then glanced up at his favorite deputy.

Vail rubbed the pulsing vein of one temple as though on the verge of a man killer of a headache, then said, " 'Fore you start bitchin' and growlin' 'bout not gettin' the entire week off like I promised, Custis, be aware that I wouldn't have sent for you unless it was absolutely necessary. Fear sending for you just could not be avoided."

Longarm squirmed deeper into the well-broken-in seat of Vail's serenely comfortable leather guest chair. Of a sudden, it occurred to him that he actually loved that chair. There'd been times in the past when he'd damned near fell asleep sitting in it. Yes, on more than one occasion, he'd nearly nodded off while only half-assed listening to Billy Vail rant and rave at him for some perceived, or actual, transgression—usually some unintentional sin committed in pursuance of bad men, or bad women, in bad places.

Long ran appreciative fingers over some of the brass-headed tacks on the front of one of the cozy seat's arms, and wondered if, just perhaps, he could talk Vail into giving him the exceptionally restful chair some day. He knew the exact spot where it would best fit in the roadside-trash decor of his less than palatial rented digs on Denver's Cherry Creek. My God, he thought, I could sleep like a newborn babe in this thing. In a flash, Longarm realized beyond any doubt that he'd easily sleep a hell of a lot better in Billy Vail's leather chair than in that bag of rocks his landlady called a bed. All he had to do was figure out a way to get Billy to part with it.

Sounding falsely magnanimous, Longarm finally brought his mind back to whatever the subject at hand would eventually become, glanced up at the U.S. marshal, then said, "Aw, hell, Billy, that's okay. But I think you should know, by God, you did in fact interrupt what appeared to be workin' into the most incredible sexual experience of my entire adult life—up to this point."

Vail's head rolled back as though his neck had suddenly turned to a stalk of rubber. "Oh, Jesus, give me comfort."

"No kiddin' here, paid. No, sir, not in the least. We're talkin' 'bout a once-in-a-lifetime event involving two of the most beautiful women in Denver—at the same time. Women capable of doing all the things you ever envisioned in your wildest daydreams. Yes, indeed, old friend, you snatched me away from an episode of such hedonistic munificence as to border on the carnally historical. And, I might add, one that may never come my way again. Breaks my heart just thinkin' 'bout what I'm missin' 'cause of you."

Vail rolled bloodshot eyes toward heaven, then let his chin drop to his chest. "Merciful Father above," he growled. "Guess I shoulda known, but you've gotta trust me on this one, Custis. I wasn't kidding when I said I was eternally grateful you ran Wolf Magruder to ground out on the Jornada del Muerto a month ago, and you know it. And I meant every word of it when I said you could, and should, take an entire week to relax, recover, and recuperate. I'm well aware that any man who leads the kind of day-to-day life you do needs his recreation."

"Well, by God, you should still be thankin' me for trackin' ole Wolf down like I did, Billy. Yes, indeed. Not many men would have gone at the task with such devotion, given where I had to go. Jornada del Muerto's gotta be the most desolate piece of acreage in the entirety of New Mexico Territory, if you ask me. And even if you don't ask me."

"From your report on the chase—of which, by the way, I have read every word—sounded to me as though you had a bitch of a time out there."

Longarm grunted and arched an eyebrow. "Bitch of a time don't even come close to describing a ride into the Jornada del Muerto, Billy. Wouldn't wish such a trip on my worst enemy, and hope, by God, never to go back to that devilish place again. Fact is, the U.S. government don't come nowhere near to payin' me enough for a return trip through that hellhole for any reason I can begin to imagine."

Vail waved as though swatting at a nuisance insect, then growled, "Yeah, yeah, yeah. I hear you. I hear you. Life's hard all around these days, Custis, and you know it.

"Ain't kiddin', Billy. I am thoroughly convinced that the Lord woke up on an eighth and heretofore unrecorded day of the Creation and decided to build a spot on Earth that was hotter'n hell under an iron skillet. A sandblasted, waterless, horror story. A plot of desolation especially designed for bitin' lizards, Gila monsters, and rattlesnakes of every sort and variety. Along with hairy-legged spiders the size of a Mexican's sombrero, sand flies, fleas, and every other kind of irritatin' insect known to man. Hell, the Jornada del Muerto's the closest thing to actual smokin', sulfurous perdition on this Earth that I've ever seen or had to ride across."

Vail acted as though he hadn't heard so much as a word of Long's rambling tirade. He seemed almost wistful when he said, "Too bad you couldn't have brought Magruder back alive. Sure would like to have witnessed his hanging."

"Hell, wasn't my fault. Stupid bastard didn't have sense enough to take ten times more water'n he needed for a dumb-assed trip into that appalling, hundred-mile stretch of wasteland. True enough, long as we were just a bit south of Albuquerque and skirtin' the foothills of the Los Pinos

Mountains wasn't much of a problem. Soon as that idiot turned into the Jornada . . . well, suffice to say he was nothin' more'n a dead man ridin' a dead horse. Worse, though, a time or two I thought he was gonna take me to the other side with him."

Vail leaned over the chaotic stack of legal briefs, file folders, and sundry other papers heaped on his desk. He scratched around a bit, then shook his head as though in resignation at not being able to find something in particular. He said, "Seems I remember, from your report, that you actually did find his body, though. That right?"

"Yeah. You know, Billy, not sure how he did it, but that dumb-as-a-stump piece of murderin' trash made it all the way through the Lava Gate to a spot called Laguna del Muerto. Got there just in time to discover the lake was drier'n a bullfrog under a cabbage leaf. Deader'n hell in a preacher's front parlor when I finally found all that was left of 'im. Tongue black as coal and big as a saddlebag. Horse, too. Coyotes, wolves, and other such scavengers had already been at both corpses. 'Course, I couldn't bring ole Wolf back. Damn sure couldn't bring the horse."

Vail missed the joke. From behind pinched eyebrows, he said, "Bury 'im?"

"Hell, no, I didn't bury the big son of a bitch. Sweet Christ. If I'd dug a hole that size in the Jornada's kinda heat, probably woulda sweated out enough to refloat ole Noah's boat."

"Uh, sorry, I just wasn't thinkin' straight."

"Left the murderin' sack of stink layin' where he fell. By now, probably ain't nothin' remainin' of the evil skunk— well, maybe a pile of sun-bleached bones. But I'll tell you the gospel truth, Billy, given the horrors of the Jornada, it's a wonder I ain't layin' out there in the hot sand right beside him. Know one thing for sure, by God. If'n I hadn't carried enough water for a whole company of deputy marshals, me'n my animal would've died sure as pissants cain't pull boxcars."

"Well, as I said when you came in, appreciate the effort and wouldn't wish a trip to that godforsaken piece of killer desert on any democrat I've ever met. But, as you well know, that's the way the job shakes out sometimes. Right now, we've got an emergency situation at hand, and I need the best man I've got on it."

Deputy Marshal Custis Long sat up in his seat and leaned forward. He and his boss almost always did a bit of friendly sparring over Longarm's difficulties while on past assignments, his inability to get enough time off after a particularly difficult task, or his efforts to service the entire female population of Colorado and most of the surrounding states and territories. But whatever had hold of Vail at that particular moment appeared more than a bit serious. For the first time ever, Long realized that Marshal Billy Vail actually appeared stricken.

"Well, what the hell's the problem, Billy? Come on, spit it out. Can't be that bad."

"George Brackett and Junior Pelts are dead, Custis."

The news of two deputy marshals falling in the line of duty at the same time dropped on Custis Long like an anvil pitched from heaven's front doorstep. For a second he couldn't believe what he'd just heard. Damned fine men, the pair of them. Now they were both gone. Nothing more than a rapidly fading set of memories. Dead as a couple of rotten hoe handles.

"Jesus Christ, Billy, the both of 'em?"

"Yes. Two of my finest deputy marshals, and they're deader'n a pair of six-card poker hands at the same table."

Long wagged his head like an old, extremely tired dog.

"Sweet Virginia, if that don't beat all. Where'd it happen? When and how?"

"Poor boys got killed a week or so ago, near as I can figure. Or, hell, maybe as much as two weeks ago. Tell the God's truth, I'm not really sure. Bodies turned up a few miles this side of Amarillo. Down south near the Palo Duro River. 'Course all that information's based on some highly sketchy telegraph messages sent to me by local law in the damn-near-nonexistent burg of Mesquite. Just gotta figure local boys, like them as sent the wire, are 'bout as dependable as a bunch of three-legged horses."

"Amarillo? That the hole in the ground a bit east of Tascosa they used to call Oneida?"

"The very same."

"Hell, Billy, there ain't nothin' out there but a Denver, Texas & Fort Worth Railroad depot house, some cattle pens, maybe a post office, and a few businesses. Tascosa ain't much. And ever since the cattle drives started to fall off year by year, the pitiful place's dyin' on the vine. But, God Almighty, right now Amarillo's the biggest goose egg in all of the great Lone Star State. What in the blue-eyed hell were George and Junior doin' out in the middle of Nowhere, Texas?"

Vail hung his head, sniffed, then picked at the corner of one eye. "I put 'em out on the scout in an effort to bring Simon Grimm in for suitable trial and hanging. 'Pears as how Grimm must've got the better of them."

For a second Longarm didn't recognize the name. Then a glimmer of recollection flickered somewhere in the fertile folds of his churning brain. "Grimm? Ain't he that murderin' son of a bitch what killed an entire family of farmers over on the Green River in Utah Territory? Murdered feller was some kinda former government agent or somethin'. Retired

23

and liked livin' as far from civilization as he could get, as I remember."

"The very one, Custis. We got brought into that particular unfortunate situation because local law enforcement requested our presence. Same thing with George and Junior's murders. Town marshal of Mesquite has been cryin' like a teething baby on the tit in his missives to me. Not at all sure the man can handle the situation. Nope, not by a damned sight."

"Damn. You know, I heard as how that murderin' son of a bitch, Grimm, dispatched eight of them poor folks. Man, his wife, and six kids. Four little girls in the bunch, I think. All of 'em under the age of ten if memory serves. Would seem as how just about any town lawman of Pissant, Texas, would have a problem with a murderer like Grimm."

Vail planted his elbows atop the rubbishlike stack of paper on his desk. He lowered his head into cupped hands, then sat for several seconds without speaking a word. Finally he leaned back in his chair, cast a doleful glance over at Longarm, and said, "Bet you didn't hear how Grimm did those Green River killings, did you? 'Course not. Couldn't have. Everyone with any kind of authority tried their level best to hush up the worst of what happened. Didn't want the reality of the mess getting out to the public."

Longarm thumped the rowel of one spur. Six-pointed star twirled and jingled. "Murder's nothin' but murder, far as I'm concerned, Billy. What's so special 'bout the way Grimm went and killed them poor folks?"

"Special's not exactly the word I'd use, but there was something a mite ghoulish about the killings. Yeah, suppose you could describe them as ghoulish without stretching much."

"Ghoulish? Odd choice of words. Hell's etnernal bells, that sounds damned ominous, Billy."

Vail ran a hand from his rapidly balding pate down across his face, then rubbed a stubble-covered chin. "Big son of a bitch chopped each and every one of them into four equal pieces with a double-bit ax."

Longarm's head lolled onto the padded back of the chair. "God Almighty, have mercy," he groaned. "Are you joshin' with me, Billy? Chopped 'em up with an ax—for real and true?"

Oh, that's not the worst of it, Custis," Vail said as he rose and stepped to the window behind his desk. With one finger he parted the curtains and stared down into the busy, snow-dusted thoroughfare of Colfax Avenue. Longarm barely heard his boss when Vail muttered, "Once he'd managed to chop 'em into something like manageable enough pieces, crazy bastard made a heapin' mound outta those poor folks and set 'em ablaze."

Custis Long sat bolt upright in his chair as though a ghost had walked by and slapped the bejabbers out of him. "Burned 'em up? God Almighty. I never heard nothin' like that concernin' those killings. Once heard a wild-assed tale 'bout some evil skunks over in the Indian Territories what nailed a jury box fulla people to trees and such, then set 'em on fire. You sure 'bout Grimm, Billy? He burned those poor folks?"

"Like I said, everyone who had anything to do with investigating the Green River murders was sworn to secrecy. We wanted that particular piece of information kept secret. Figured as how, when we finally caught up with Grimm, tale of the actual events could be used to our advantage during his prosecution." After a second's silence he added, "There were other rumors about the killings as well, but in my estimation they're not worth repeating."

"What rumors?"

Vail stared at his fingers. He picked at one nail with his

thumb, then chewed at whatever he'd found. Once finished with the clumsy manicure, Vail barely spoke loud enough for Longarm to hear. "Like I said, none of it's worth repeating. But some said he did unspeakable things to those little girls before he killed them. Made each sister watch heinous acts, in turn, before killing them like butchered animals." Vail shook his head, then sighed. His voice trailed away into a whisper when he said, "Insanities so horrible they aren't worth repeating."

Longarm gritted his teeth. His back molars made a sound like ten pins falling. "Christ on a crutch. Glad you told me that last part. Well, not glad, but . . . well, you know. Helps to know something like that when you have to face a crazed killer like Grimm."

As though tired, Vail waved an arm toward his clerk's office. "Already booked you a seat on this afternoon's Denver, Texas & Fort Worth Railroad's day coach to Amarillo. It's a two-day trip from here. Want you to head on out that way, then get on down to Mesquite as quick as you can. Should be able to make it in three days, three and a half at the most. Check in with Marshal Talbot Butterworth once you get there. Promised him I'd send my best man, so he's expecting a U.S. marshal and should be able to point you in the right direction."

"And?"

Billy Vail stared at the stamped-tin ceiling of his office for several seconds. Ran a sweaty hand from thinning hair to chin again, then said, "Knowing full well that Grimm's got a week or more's worth of head start, want you to run the man to ground, then bring him back to Denver for a quick trial and even quicker hanging. Don't care how rough you have to get to do the job, Custis. In fact, if he resists, and you can just about bet he will, then kill the hell out of the murderous son of a bitch."

Longarm smiled, snatched his hat off the floor, socked it onto his head, then stood. "Anything else you think I should know before I leave, Billy?"

Vail studied the back of his hand for a moment. "Well, there is one thing that might help. That is if you feel the need. There's an old acquaintance of mine who lives somewhere around Amarillo. You might have to do some checking around to find him, but he's there somewhere. Last I heard he had a small ranch out on Wild Horse Mesa. Name's Amos Black."

"Amos Black?"

"Yeah. Probably knows more about the panhandle area of Texas than anybody living. And, perhaps more important, he's meaner'n a box of teased rattlesnakes. Figure you two should get along famously."

Long flashed a half smile, then said, "Anything else?"

For some reason, Longarm noticed, Vail didn't look up when he said, "No, Custis. Figure as how if there's anything wayward I might not have thought to mention, you'll find out about it sooner or later anyway. To tell the absolute truth, some of what came over the wires from Butterworth didn't make any sense. You'll just have to check it all out yourself when you get there."

Longarm turned on his heel and headed for the door. With fingers curled around the heavy, knurled-brass knob he heard his boss call out, "Be careful with this one, Custis. If Grimm isn't the craziest son of a bitch in Texas right now, he's damned sure nibblin' at the edges. Don't give him an inch."

"You know you don't have to worry 'bout me, Billy."

"No kiddin', Custis. Go about your business armed to the teeth, and keep your wits about you. Looney bastard's already killed at least ten people that we know of, for certain sure. Two of them poor dead folks were lawmen with twenty-five years of man-hunting experience between the pair of 'em. So, if I was you, wouldn't be surprised by anything else weird or contrary you discover about the murdering skunk along the way."

Longarm tapped the butt of his Frontier model Colt with one finger and grinned. "Trust me, Billy. Given the slightest chance to get Grimm in my sights, I'll put 'im down like the mad dog he is."

Travel documents and letters of introduction in hand, Longarm took the stairs down to the first floor two at a time. Beneath the covered portico of Denver's Federal Building, he paused, pulled a nickel cheroot from his jacket pocket, and stoked it to smoldering life. A quick glance to the west revealed an eerie, yellowish red bank of clouds moving over the Front Range of the Rockies. Strange, he thought, don't think I've ever seen a sky that color this time of day, or any other time of day for that matter. Looks almost like dried blood.

Not one for omens, premonitions, or portents, Longarm shook his head and heeled it for the street. But as he hoofed his way west along Colfax Avenue's drab sandstone sidewalk toward Cherry Creek, an icy chill grabbed him by the spine. Creeping ripples of gooseflesh raced up his back, then stopped in a tight, bunched knot between his hunched shoulder blades. To his surprise the feeling began to crawl around like something alive.

He drew up in mid-stride and glanced over his shoulder as though fully expecting to see something horrible following a few steps away. "Damn," he said to himself. "Gotta get a grip. Nothin' to this. Just another manhunt." But then the blackened images of George Brackett and Junior Pelts, chopped into pieces and being rendered into greasy fat, flashed across the back of his eyes unbidden. "Shit," he growled. "What a way to die."

Chapter 3

A bit south of Pueblo, Colorado, Longarm shifted his aching, bony behind in the ass-numbing, uncomfortable, and barely padded seat of the Denver, Texas & Fort Worth Railroad's day coach. The train's thirty-five-ton, smoke-belching, Baldwin locomotive chugged away at the head of a string of cars and had a full head of steam up.

The entire bone-rattling shebang plummeted south and east at the eye-popping speed of twenty-five miles an hour. Longarm could feel the shudder and click of the glistening steel rails beneath his feet. A reassuring jangle oozed up through the thinly padded seat, along the entirety of his jostling tail bone all the way to the fillings in his back teeth.

The magnificent view of the Front Range of the Rocky Mountains slid by Longarm's window barely noticed. Years of riding those ribbons of iron in pursuit of murderers, thieves, and brigands of every stripe had caused the cramp-muscled lawdog to grow somewhat callous to the spectacular scene of grandeur that loomed above the horizon little more than twenty miles to the west.

In the early days of his tenure as a lawman, he'd truly reveled in the required travel. A lengthy train ride was just his cup of tea. The whole experience tended to relax him before the tension of the hunt finally set in. And he enjoyed the company of the other passengers. Went out of his way to speak with them and exchange pleasantries. As succeeding years passed, piled one upon another, train travel became far more mundane and eventually nothing more than a tiresome but necessary part of the job. A part of the job that, by now, had grown more than a bit tedious and, in all but the most unusual cases, downright wearisome.

Near as Longarm could recall, the vast majority of the travelers he met—in the beginning of his lengthy career as a lawdog—were of the highest quality. Most times, they were well-dressed, energetic, educated, moneyed people with a purpose. Back in those halcyon days, his fellow passengers were those who could afford the somewhat prohibitive expense of a ticket. Now it appeared that any sort of trash imaginable could easily come up with the required toll for a trip to the backside of the most inaccessible spots in the West. As a consequence of that realization, he tended to keep to himself and tried his level best to avoid speaking with any of his fellow voyagers, unless absolutely necessary.

Worn near to a frazzle by the previous night's romp with Cora and the talented Minnie, Longarm had hoofed it from Billy Vail's office to his Cherry Creek digs and got himself outfitted in less than an hour. He'd arrived at the depot in a dead run and barely made it onto an already moving train for an earlier departure than originally scheduled.

Breathing like a winded racehorse, he'd flopped onto a seat near a window that faced in the direction of the train's progress. There was just something uncomfortable about looking out at places he'd already been instead of where he was going. That had never set well with Longarm. In an effort to keep other passengers at arm's length, if possible, he'd also taken the seat directly across from him for his mound of guns, saddlebags, equipment, and other necessaries.

Upon the train's chuffing departure from the Denver depot, a quick glance around had revealed a sparsely occupied coach. The weary lawman had counted a grand total of only ten other riders. Four of those were members of a single family comprised of a snaggle-toothed, tired-to-the-bone gent dressed in the rough garb of a farmer; his pinch-faced, calico-draped, wizened wife; and two rambunctious tow-headed wall climbers.

A pair of loud, talkative, uniformed cavalry grunts, obviously on leave, occupied a seat near the back of the car and passed an unlabeled, open, amber-colored bottle of hard liquor back and forth. The largest, and most brutish-looking, of the soldiers appeared to have been at the bottle for days. Neither man's whiskey-soaked, bloodshot eyes seemed capable of focusing on much of anything. In the few seconds that Longarm watched the pair, the big man almost fell out of his seat twice.

Tired, down-at-the-heel, sad-faced drummers of various sorts, in battered hats and frayed suits, made up the rest of the tiny company of passengers. Much to Longarm's relief, none of them appeared any too anxious for company or idle conversation.

In Pueblo a stately looking lady, wearing the severe black hat and garb of recent widowhood, came aboard. With a youngster in tow, she took a seat almost directly across the aisle from the farm couple and their insufferable pair of patch-assed kids.

The widow was followed aboard by a rough-looking hombre dressed in the coarse buckskin clothing of a working buffalo hunter. Along with a .50-caliber Sharps rifle, he lugged down the aisle a pile of something covered in skins that smelled to high heaven.

The putrid reek, wafting off the buffalo man and his pungent load, came nigh on to knocking Longarm out of his chosen spot. As best he could, the gagging lawman used his hat to fan the nose-twisting odor away. The stench proved more than enough to put a pack of buzzards off their feed. Long raised his eyes to heaven and said silent thanks to a beneficent God as the odiferous skunk headed to the last bench in the car before finally taking a seat.

In an effort to further banish the hunter's lingering bouquet of polecat, Longarm fished a fresh cheroot from his jacket pocket, then stoked it to life. He watched as the thin line of bluish gray smoke curled toward the coach's ceiling, then slipped out a tiny opening at the top of the window. In the open air, the wispy cloud quickly trailed from the passenger car and blended with the thick black rope of burned coal dust that poured from the chugging engine's massive stack, slid back toward the caboose, then vanished.

As no females who looked unattached had come aboard, Longarm pulled his Stetson down over his eyes and attempted to take a much-needed nap. For a second, he wondered if, perhaps, the unmarried women might be on the other passenger coach. Such thoughts didn't last long, though. Within minutes of covering his face, the rocking of the car and *clickety clack* of the rails lulled him to sleep. Debauched visions of Cora Anne and her hot-tailed, blond-haired *complice de l'amour* snatched him out of his reveries on several occasions, before he finally drifted into a deep, satisfying snooze.

From somewhere midway between Pueblo and Trinidad, he nodded and napped until a noisy disagreement broke out between the stately looking lady's evil progeny and one of the kids across the aisle. From beneath his hat brim, Longarm watched as the rowdy ruckus grew louder and more strident. It appeared as though the farm couple's shirt-tailed banty rooster had smacked the stately lady's kid in the mouth for some obscure reason. Her brat sported a swollen, bleeding lip, and weepy eyes. The adults now had their feathers ruffled like a trio of angry setters and cluckers looking for a scrap.

"I'd trust you to keep that hateful imp of yours away from my son," the stately lady snarled at the farmer's wife. Then she snatched her howling, snot-nosed child by the collar and sat him down into the seat beside her.

"Hateful imp? Did you call my son a hateful imp?" the farmer's worn-out-looking wife snapped.

The stately lady fanned herself with a lace hanky. "I do not believe I misspoke, madame," she growled. "You would be well served to take my freely offered advice."

The red-faced farmer's wife jerked a ratty, checkered shawl closer around her bony shoulders, then hopped to her feet. With a look that would have peeled paint off a barn door, she snarled, "Don't call me *madame*, you smart-mouthed trollop. A big behaver like that monster of yours needs his backside strapped more often, if you ask me. Since it appears your man is no longer among the living and most likely slashed his own throat, my husband would be more than happy to accomplish the deed for you. Few licks with his belt should remedy the situation just fine, I'd wager."

The farmer hung his head, looking stricken and more than a bit embarrassed. Longarm shook his head and, in spite of himself, felt a wave of sympathetic sorrow for the poor henpecked fellow.

Before a grown man could spit, the stately lady was on

her canoe-sized feet. She stepped across the narrow aisle and slapped the farmer's wan, bony-assed wife. The lick hit the farmer lady's jaw like a clap of thunder.

Longarm shook his head. He wondered if the pinch-faced woman's great-great-great grandpa might not have felt the open-palmed blow in a grave somewhere back in Missouri, Arkansas, Tennessee, or wherever in hell her dirt-poor, sod-busting ancestors were most likely buried.

The stately lady's sternly delivered rap across the woman's thin-lipped mouth really ripped the rag off the bush. Before a fat minnow could swim a dipper of water, the women had gone to scratching and hissing like a pair of rattlesnakes tied up in a gunnysack. The stately lady grabbed the farmer gent's shabby wife by the hair and, in about a heartbeat and a half, both women were atop the surprised farmer and were flailing at each other like a pair of crazed windmills.

The cavalry boys went to hooting and hollering their drunken encouragement. The moose-sized lout of the pair supported the farmer's wife. His smaller, perhaps a bit more sober, friend yelped, laughed, and drunkenly called out his backing for her much larger, taller, more aggressive attacker. The smelly buffalo hunter appeared only mildly amused, and most of the drummers just wagged their heads in weary disgust and disbelief like a pack of indifferent dogs.

"Jesus," Longarm grunted under his breath. "What'n the hell's the world comin' to? Bone-tired feller cain't even get a bit of sleep on a train these days 'thout a bunch of inconsiderate folks gettin' into a noisy cuss match, angry fallin'-out, or face-scratchin' hen fight of some kind."

For no readily apparent reason and to Longarm's amazed satisfaction, the disagreement suddenly appeared to slacken

34

a bit. But as the toothless kid liked to say about his birthday cake, it didn't last.

The stately lady seemed to have won the difference of opinion and headed back to her seat. She had made it about midway across the aisle when the farmer's wife surged up behind her unsuspecting adversary and whacked her across the back of her bun-covered head with a canvas travel bag big enough to secrete an anvil, a bucket full of rocks, and a couple of old McClellan cavalry saddles.

Quicker than a winter wind could lift a dead leaf, the tussle fired up again. The stricken farmer tried his best to step between the scrapping, hair-pulling women, but got slapped back into his seat. The yelping kids danced around the adults with all the abandonment of screaming, blood-thirsty Indians. They whooped, hollered, screeched, and cried like the Second Coming and the Rapture were surely at hand.

In a disapproving voice, more than loud enough to be heard by everyone in the car, Longarm finally snarled, "For the love of God, you women give it a rest. Christ's sake, a man can't even take a nap on a movin' train 'thout bein' kept awake by a ridiculous fracas over misbehaving yard apes."

One of the agitating cavalrymen, the largest, drunkest, and clearly most aggressive of the pair, yelled, "Aw, shut the hell up, you ugly son of a bitch. Let 'em fight it out. This here's better'n any distraction I've come on since the night I watched a buncha nekkid gals bowl ten pins in a Hell's Half Acre joint down in Fort Worth. Maybe these 'uns here'll get to rasslin' 'round and show us their knickers. Jus' ain't nothin' like a good catfight, fer as I'm concerned." He elbowed his more diminutive buddy. They both snorted out liquor-saturated guffaws.

Longarm turned and shot a slit-eyed glare at the mouthy pair of horse apples.

The big trooper glared back, shook his half-empty bottle at Longarm, then said, "You sure's hell don't want to be lookin' at me like that, mister. Just might have to climb up outta this here butt-numbin' seat. Kick yer skinny ass till yer nose bleeds, by God."

The bearish soldier's runty friend, who'd hit the bottle so hard during the scuffle he was now obviously drunker than a waltzing pissant, mumbled, " 'At's right. Bes' shut on the hell up miz-zer, 'fore we have to get up and kick the hell outta yer lanky ass."

Longarm didn't get a chance to respond to either of the loutish cavalrymen's challenges. A pair of red-faced, mouth-breathing conductors happened on the scene and quickly set about defusing the situation. Longarm recognized one of the train's officials. He and Mike Dancer had ridden the rails east together more times than either man cared to remember. Dancer was more than competent at his job, and Longarm knew the man would quickly have the women separated and quiet again.

Sure enough, the train line's official representatives hustled right into the middle of the screeching fray. Dancer and his companion pulled the mouthy combatants apart and re-seated them far enough from each other to bring about something akin to muttering peace. Didn't matter to Longarm a sense of palpable tension still hung in the coach's fetid air.

Rather than suffer an unwanted confrontation with the drunken cavalry troopers, he decided to take his gear and head for the second coach and the possibility of a more peaceable, relaxing ride. Hell, there may be female company back there. Didn't really matter, though at least he'd be away from the yelping and the drunks.

Loaded down with all his gear, he managed to make it

past the glowering louts at the back of the car and into the train's second passenger coach with no further incident. Much to his relief, the swaying car was even more sparsely populated than the first, but there were no women on it either. He confiscated a pair of seats near the front and, in no time at all, drifted off to sleep again.

Chapter 4

Ten hours after witnessing the catfight, Longarm dragged himself onto the Denver, Texas & Fort Worth Railroad's Amarillo loading platform. The windswept, treeless, uninhabited terrain for miles around in every direction reminded him way too much of the Jornada del Muerto. Worse, he knew that Amarillo was the absolute garden spot of the entire area. And, even worse still, he harbored no doubts that if his business took him south, the landscape would grow more barren and difficult with each plodding, sunbaked step.

He dropped his pile of gear on the platform and proceeded to light a cheroot. After firing the finger-sized stogie, he shook the match to death and flipped it onto the gravel edge of the tracks several feet below the level of the passenger's loading platform. He couldn't believe his eyes when the pair of booze-saturated cavalrymen stumbled off the train and ominously started wobbling his direction.

The inebriated soldiers staggered down the dock, then swayed to a stop a few steps away. Looked as though they'd refreshed their liquor supply. Each man held a recently opened bottle of hundred-fifty-proof panther sweat clasped in filthy fingers.

The largest, more bullish trooper pointed at Longarm with his booze-filled hand, then growled, "Got a bone to pick with you, asshole. Thought I'd fergot about ya, didn't ya. Well, I don't never fergit a slight from assholes like you. Went and eyeballed me in just the exact wrong way, by God. Ain't no man goes eyeballin' mc like you done 'thout gittin' a lickin'."

Longarm held his hands up in the universal gesture of peace. "Look, I don't want any trouble with either of you fellers. Didn't mean to offend. You have my sincerest apology. Hope we can just forget the whole affair and go our separate ways."

"Fuck yer 'sincerest' fuckin' apology. Yer due a beatin', bud. Had neither the time nor the inclination to whip yer stringy ass whilst we was on this here train. Didn't want to offend them conductors, ya see. Have to get myself to Fort Worth and can't afford to get kicked off the rattlin' fucker. But now, by God, your time has come. I'm gonna whip the shit out'n yer tall-drink-a-water ass. I'm gonner rub yer face in 'at shit, then catch the next train on south. Laugh like a son of a bitch all the way to Fort Worth."

More than a bit bemused, Longarm shook his head, grinned, and watched as the stubble-faced ruffian handed his recently opened bottle to his swaying friend. Then the belligerent jackass proceeded to try to peel off a service jacket that appeared about two sizes smaller than he needed.

The way Longarm had the situation figured, if he ended the whole dance by simply shooting the ignorant wretch in the head, the poor son of a bitch would have to sober up just to go on and die.

Several times during the grunting trooper's never-ending attempt to disrobe, he wobbled, stumbled, and almost fell off the loading platform. His drunken, weasely friend, while attempting to hold a whiskey bottle in each hand, tried his best

40

to help by pulling at his gargantuan partner's clinging sleeve with one or two unused fingers. The clumsy maneuver only made the entire situation worse. Both of the intoxicated ruffians lurched into a baggage cart and came near to knocking the contraption onto its side. Their grunting, yelling, and cursing began to draw a small but inquisitive crowd of curious men and women.

At some point, the larger of the two yobs waved one enormous arm just the wrong way. He managed to smack his buddy across the arm, and his very own bottle slipped from the smaller trooper's questionable grip. The glass container hit the surface of the loading dock and burst into a jillion whiskey-covered, amber-colored, glittery glass fragments. For several odd, silent seconds, the drunks stood over the remains of the fractured jug as though it was the body of a recently murdered comrade.

Of a sudden, the bigger man went into a slobbering fit of teeth-gritting rage. He turned on his friend and yelped, "Gawdamn it, Reggie. Which 'un wuz that? Whose bottle you done went and busted? Clumsy son of a bitch."

Reggie stared at the glassy mess with slowly blinking eyes and said, "That 'un wuz yern, Clyde. Sorry, but I wouldn'ta dropped 'er, if'n you hadn't a bumped into me. Big, lumberin' bastard. Always been clumsier'n a three-legged cow. Swear 'fore Jesus, Clyde, I think you could fall yore big ass *up* a well without even tryin'."

Longarm crossed his arms as an uncontrollable grin etched its way across his face. He took a step back and waited for what he knew, without doubt, was on its way. The mindless drunken ire that had recently been pointed his direction suddenly took, for poor Reggie at least, an unexpected and comical turn.

Clyde, the monster cavalry trooper, glared at his smaller friend. His neck swelled as though he was about to snatch the smaller man's head off and render it a pulpy mess. A paw the size of a camp skillet flicked between them and slapped at Reggie's bottle. The container flew out of the runt's grasp, hit the depot's rugged, rough-cut board flooring, and shattered in a loud pop of glass fragments and splattering nose paint. A goodly amount of the wondrous liquid rained down on the boots of several giggling bystanders.

Reggie staggered over to the pool of wasted panther sweat, bent down, almost fell, then snatched up the jagged bottle neck from the pile of ruined glass that crunched beneath his booted feet. He turned on the wobbling giant like a cornered, snarling bobcat. He waved the chunk of glistening glass and screeched, "Stupid pile of hammered dog shit. Tole you I 'uz sorry. No reason to do what you jus' done, Clyde. No fuckin' reason a'tall."

"Shoulda helt on to my jug better, Reggie. Shouldn'ta dropped it like you done."

"You knocked it out'n my hand, you clumsy, ass-suckin' bastard. Now you gone and broke my jug on purpose. Big stupid cocksucker." Then little Reggie jumped at the larger man and slashed him across the neck with the serrated chunk of his destroyed bottle's neck.

The consequences of Reggie's assault were instantaneous. A ribbon of bright red blood squirted into the air and sprayed across the smaller man's twisted, grinning, hysterical countenance. Droplets from the ragged incision flew onto the shirts, coats, and dresses of several of the surprised bystanders.

Clyde yelped like a kicked dog, then clamped a massive paw over the new mouthlike opening in his neck. A river of gore leaked from between grabbling fingers. The big man sounded like a wounded bear when he howled, "Gawd damn, Reggie. You done went and cut my fuckin' throat. Runty son of a bitch. Jesus, you mighta done went and kilt me, for Christ's sake."

From somewhere inside his tunic, Reggie's massive companion fumbled around and somehow retrieved another unopened jug. Before the smaller man's whiskey-saturated brain could even begin thinking of how to respond, Clyde whacked him across the face. The still-sealed bottle shattered against Reggie's nose in a cloud of splintered shards and flying liquid. Whiskey and glass went in a thousand different directions at the same time.

Little Reggie's head twisted around on his stalklike neck as though it might snap completely off. Blood spurted across the loading platform in a ropy stream. A hand-sized splattering of droplets almost landed on Longarm's freshly shined boots. The surprised, miniature trooper let out a strange yelping squeak, then went down to one knee and grabbed his near-severed beak. He glanced at his bloody hand, then quickly latched onto the damaged honker again.

With blood-drenched fingers covering most of his face and mouth, it was hard for anyone in the gathering crowd of laughing, pointing gawkers to understand him, when Reggie cried out, "Damnation, Clyde, you done come nigh on to amputatin' my snout. Sliced right through the bony part what holds it all together. Nothin' keepin' 'er on now but a fingernail-sized strip a meat. Big, stupid cocksucker."

One hand still clamped to his gushing neck, the mountainous Clyde grinned like a thing insane. He waved the razor-sharp remnants of the shattered bottle in his friend's face, then growled, "Well, now you know how it feels, doncha, Reggie. Guess I'll have to do better next time, you stupid little shit. Take that there bulbous glob a gristle off'n yer face altogether. Maybe gouge out one a yer eyes as well. Rip off an ear. Teach you to go droppin' my hard-earned bottle a tarantula piss."

Longarm watched as Reggie's hand slipped down into the top of his stovepipe serviceman's boot. His fingers came

43

out wrapped around a thin-pointed blade that bore a striking resemblance to a flattened, razor-sharp railroad spike with a fancy ivory and silver handle attached to it. Before ole big-assed, inattentive Clyde could wipe the stupid, mocking grin off his face, the smaller man raised the knife above his head, then squealed like a wounded pig.

At almost the same instant, the train's engineer blew several short blasts on his whistle to announce the Denver, Texas & Fort Worth Railroad's continuation of its route south and east. Released steam from the chuffing locomotive rolled down the loading platform in a dense, white, hissing cloud. As the vaporized water enveloped him, Reggie leapt into the air like his feet were attached to coiled steel springs. Longarm watched in wordless amazement as the screaming man flew into the roiling mist and appeared to vanish.

Next thing Longarm knew, when the watery cloud had begun to thin a bit, Clyde stumbled sidewise out of the rising haze and crab-walked dangerously close to the edge of the depot's loading dock. Reggie's nasty-looking blade was buried in the big man's heaving upper chest—all the way down to its shiny, brass hilt.

Clyde gasped for air, clawed his shirt open, grabbed at the knife's fancy ivory handle, and jerked on it several times. A confused, panicked look spread over his twisted face when nothing happened. The blade appeared immovable. Wild-eyed, Clyde wrestled with the life-draining instrument, stumbled, and suddenly went over backward and disappeared onto the tracks below.

Standing but a few feet away from the tragic action, Longarm rushed to the edge of the loading dock. He glanced down just in time to watch as wheel after wheel of the passing railroad cars rolled across the middle of the big man's sizable body.

Longarm snatched his hat off and shielded his eyes from the stunning horror only a few feet below. Nothing he could do but turn away as quickly as possible. He strode back to his mounded pile of belongings and hoped that the night's dreams wouldn't be filled with repeated viewings of the scene that had taken place not ten feet from the tips of his boots.

Screeching women and yelling men ran about the depot's passenger and freight loading platform like crazed, headless birds. One fellow kept enough presence of mind to start out on a useless run to flag the engineer down and stop the moving train. Of course his well-intentioned efforts proved totally fruitless. The southbound chain of heavy cars built up speed with each successive plunge of the Baldwin's drive rod. Every wheel of at least one passenger car, the express car, three freight cars, half a dozen empty cattle cars, and the caboose rolled over Clyde's halved remains. Longarm would later recall seeing a brakeman standing on the back landing of the caboose, hat in hand, scratching his head as he tried to figure out what had just happened.

Amarillo's station agent, a pale, nervous, mousy little man wearing a green shade over his eyes, damn near came unhinged. He had not a hair on his head, but appeared to be pulling out what few strands God might have left. At one point, trembling like a weeping willow in a cyclone, the railroad's Amarillo representative turned to Longarm and moaned, "Just unbelievable. He's the third one to be run over this month. My employers will go into seizures when I inform them of this latest catastrophe."

Longarm cast a quick glance around in search of Clyde's former friend, Reggie. The little man was nowhere to be seen. Gone. Gone as surely as the wafting steam from the engine had evaporated on a dry Texas breeze. Shouldn't be hard to find him, though, Longarm thought. Hell, ole Clyde had come damn near to cutting his fucking nose off.

Amarillo's miniature, Spartan railroad depot boasted a grand total of three wooden benches for tired, waiting travelers. Painted a brilliant shade of green, their slatted bottoms offered even less comfort than the day coach's barely padded seats. An iron, potbellied woodstove, sitting in one corner of the ten-by-twelve room, appeared the only nod toward something like creature comfort. A sign over a door in the back wall advised anyone in need of the location of the outhouse. Whitewashed walls almost glowed. The floors smelled of pine sap. The ticket clerk's cagelike, barred window overlooked the austere, near-empty space.

Longarm pitched his pile of goods onto the floor, flopped onto the bench nearest the depot's doorway to the loading platform, then lit himself a smoke. He shook his head at the amazing level of gross stupidity he'd just witnessed. And he waited. No point leaving, he thought. Someone with a smattering of authority will eventually show up to investigate, and sure as all the doorknobs in hell are hot, that someone'll be looking for me.

Chapter 5

The eventual appearance of someone possessed of a degree of influence took a bit longer than Billy Vail's favorite deputy marshal expected. Longarm had smoked two of his nickel cheroots, when a stocky, bull-necked gent jingled into the railway's depot building. The man sported a bushy moustache, a palm-leaf sombrero the size of a wagon wheel, Mexican spurs with silver-mounted rowels almost as big as the hat, and an odd badge shaped like a waving flag with the word MARSHAL carved into it. Although Amarillo's round-faced lawman offered a friendly smile and nod, he flicked a wary glance at the big Frontier model Colt lying across Longarm's belly, then rested a hand on the butt of one of his own weapons.

To Longarm, the jumpy, thick-necked gent looked like he should have been traveling with a two-wagon carnival and wrestling all comers in every pissant-sized, one-dog burg in Texas. The tired deputy U.S. marshal flashed a tight, noncommittal grin, then nodded back.

The local lawdog appeared to relax a bit. He hooked both stubby thumbs behind a double-rowed, military-style canvas cartridge belt. The thick band of webbing supported a brace of walnut-gripped Smith & Wesson No. 3 Schofield revolvers. Longarm got the impression that while he looked like a wrestler or working butcher, the heavily armed badge toter just might prove extremely problematic in any kind of lead-pitching contest.

Almost apologetically, the Amarillo lawman said, "After-noon, sir. Name's Barton Wheeler. Town marshal here'bouts." In what appeared an effort to put Longarm at his ease, Wheeler placed a foot on the bench, then leaned over on one elbow. As though confessing to a priest, he said, "Well, to tell the gospel truth, friend, I only work part-time right now. We ain't got much in the way of a town yet when it comes right down to it. Sure you could easily see that when the train rolled in."

Longarm nodded again.

Wheeler persisted with his friendly lawman act by adding, "Anyhow, I 'uz talking with some of them excited folks out yonder on the loading platform. Damned upset bunch, ain't they? They 'uz tellin' me as how you were the one I needed to speak with. Said as how if you'n me palavered a bit, I just might be able to get the whole blood-soaked story of what the hell happened to that poor feller the train run over. That true?"

Longarm pulled his sheaf of bona fides out of his jacket pocket, along with the leather wallet containing his badge. He offered the whole package to Wheeler, then said, "Think you just about covered it, Marshal. Train ran over 'im. Chopped him in half like a butchered heifer in a Kansas City slaughterhouse. Made not a single sound once he hit the ground; leastways, none as I heard over the train pullin' out. Poor bastard didn't have a chance once he dropped over the edge of the loadin' dock."

Wheeler glanced at the official documents and badge, then handed them back. "Man has a big ole Arkansas toothpick stickin' outta his chest, Marshal Long. Fancy son of a bitch. Ivory grips, silver mounted. Damned nice blade. 'Pears custom made, near as I can tell. Kinda killin' instrument I wouldn't wanta leave layin' 'round. Bet it cost a right pretty penny."

"Yeah, but, you gotta admit, that ain't what killed 'im."

Wheeler shook his head and grinned. " 'Course, I know. The train. The train."

"Train wasn't exactly all of it, though. Stupidity, Marshal Wheeler. Drunken, arrogant stupidity. That's what killed Trooper Clyde—Whoever. Not sure of the liquor-saturated lout's last name. Never heard him or his friend mention any last names."

Amarillo's part-time marshal pulled a worn leather wallet from his own jacket, opened it, then said, "James Clyde Wadkins, accordin' to these here papers we found on what was left of the corpse. On leave and headed for Fort Worth, near as I've been able to ascertain."

"He said as much, not long before God came and got him. The business 'bout goin' to Fort Worth, I mean."

"Ah. I see."

"Big dumb bastard's whiskey-soaked brain got out of control. For some reason he found a prickly burr 'bout the size of a rabid weasel in the crotch of his balbriggans first time he set eyes on me. Or maybe, it was the other way around. Anyhow, Trooper Wadkins and that idiot travelin' companion of his confronted me soon as we stepped off the train from Denver. Whole dance got more than a bit confused over a bottle of wasted liquor. The troopers got in each other's faces. His friend stabbed the hell outta the poor son of a bitch. Then he went to stumblin' around, got too close to the edge of the platform, and fell off. Rest, as they say, is about as clear as a glass dinner bell."

Wheeler rubbed his stubbly chin with the back of one

hand, looked thoughtful for several seconds, then said, "You see what direction the feller what done the stabbin' went when he took off?"

Longarm shook his head. "Nope. Just disappeared. Vanished like a gob of spit on a hot stove lid during all the blood and confusion. 'Course, you shouldn't have much trouble findin' him."

"How's that?"

· "Dead man came damn near to cuttin' his honker off."

Wheeler's eyes narrowed. Of a sudden, he got the look of a man who'd just been told a hard-to-believe tale about a carnival geek whose body was covered in colorful tattoos from neck to ankles and who ate glass and pounded horseshoe nails through his tongue with a ball-peen hammer for the enjoyment of any nasty-assed hayseed with a nickel.

"No shit?" Wheeler mumbled, then gazed at the ceiling as though searching for God.

"Absolutely. Got 'im with the broken neck of a whiskey bottle. Made a helluva mess. Poor ole cut-nosed Reggie ain't gonna heal up no time in the near future, I can guarantee that. Gonna be one lucky son of a bitch if he even has a nose when his ordeal finally draws to an end. If I were you, Marshal, I'd be headin' straight for the closest doctor's office. Bet he's doin' a right diligent search for someone to sew his hooter back on."

As though still distracted, Wheeler mumbled, "Doc's outside with our local undertaker seein' to what's left of the corpse. 'S a helluva mess. Blood, guts, bone, all manner of viscera scattered around out there. Looks like hog slaughterin' time back in Georgia to me. Havin' to pick up most of the poor bastard with a rake, a long-handled shovel, and a mop bucket."

Longarm nodded in agreement, rose from the depot's murderously uncomfortable bench, and quickly gathered up his belongings. "Can you point me toward a livery, Marshal Wheeler?" he asked.

As suddenly as he'd drifted away, Wheeler came back to himself. "Ah, you here on official business, Marshal Long?"

"Yes. Yes, I am. Headed for Mesquite, as a matter of pure fact. My boss, United States Marshal Billy Vail, is hopeful local law enforcement officials down that way can put me on the trail of a killer named Simon Grimm."

As Wheeler followed Longarm back onto the loading platform, he said, "Peace officer down in Mesquite's a friend of mine. Talbot Butterworth. Good man. Sure he'll help you all he can. Grimm. Grimm. Seems like I've heard that moniker somewhere. He that crazy sonofabitch what likes to chop folks up with an ax?"

Surprised by the country lawman's knowledge, Longarm stopped in his tracks near the steps leading off the end of the loading dock. He turned and cocked his head to one side. "Yeah. That's the one. How'd you know 'bout him?"

Wheeler grinned and did an abbreviated dance as though pleased he'd said something of interest. "Oh, well, my friend Marshal Butterworth sent word by way of the stage 'tween here and there. Said the man'd committed a couple a terrible murders out on the Palo Duro River not far from town. Said I should be on the lookout for the evil skunk. Made it about as clear as a bucket of rainwater I'd best be careful if'n I ran across Grimm." Wheeler paused, then added, "Not sure of what to make of it, but there's somethin' strange 'bout them killin's. Real strange." Then as though lost in thought once again, he mumbled, "Somethin' real strange."

Expecting the man to expand on his cryptic musings, Longarm waited. When Wheeler appeared completely preoccupied and nothing more came, Longarm said, "Say, there's a stage line running between here and Mesquite, Marshal?"

"Oh, yeah. Yeah. Sure 'nuff. Lone Star Transport and Freight. Ain't much. On its last legs actually. But they still make a run to Mesquite once a day. Down in the morning, back in the afternoon."

Longarm hefted his load and shifted it to a more comfortable spot on his back. "Well, in that case, think I'll just spend the night here in town and take the stage down tomorrow morning. Rather than a livery, maybe you can point me to a decent hotel."

Wheeler grabbed his hat by the brim, lifted it off his pumpkin-shaped head, and scratched a near hairless pate with one finger. "Unfortunately, we ain't got no real honest-to-God hotels around town yet—decent or otherwise. Buildin' on a couple of 'em. Nothin' finished. Got a roomin' house. Several of 'em. Best of 'em belongs to a lady name of Maybell Dawes."

"Maybell Dawes?"

"Yeah. She'n her husband were among some a the first permanent settlers around these parts. 'Course, her poor runnin' mate passed on several years back—accordin' to them as can still remember the man. As a matter of necessity, Mrs. Dawes started takin' in one or two permanent boarders and visitin' itinerants what managed to find out about her cookin'."

"Old age kill the husband?"

"Well, he warn't no spring chicken when he went out that's for sure. But, to be truthful, the way I heard it, a diamondback rattler 'bout the size of a horse's leg jumped up'n bit 'im."

"Jesus."

Wheeler patted the side of his neck. "Yeah. Got the poor bastard right square in the jugular. Tale most folks tell goes as how he'd bent over to pull up a stick a stove wood outta the stack 'side the house. Snake musta been hid out under the kindlin' or somethin'. Once he got tagged, poor ole Dawes was dead in a matter of days. Heard tell as how his entire head swole up the size of a number three galvanized washtub, then turned blacker'n pitch. Say he 'uz outta his mind after that happened. Whole body shook and trembled like waves on the ocean for nigh on two days." Wheeler trembled all over, then did a little stutter-step dance. "Shit, gives me the goose-bumped willies just thinkin' 'bout such a death."

Longarm shook his head, then stared at the toes of his boots. "Uh-huh. Guess gettin' dosed in the jugular by a diamondback'd sure 'nuff do the trick alright."

Wheeler made an off-handed waving motion toward the end of the depot building. "Yeah, well, tell you what, Marshal Long, just go 'round front of the depot. Should be a hack driver parked out there name of Old Mike Turnipseed. Tell 'im I said to take you over to Maybell Dawes's place out by Wild Horse Lake. Clean house and good food. Eat there as often as I can myself. Mrs. Dawes'll treat you right, Marshal Long."

"Wild Horse Lake, you say?"

"Yep. Short ride. Won't take long. Twenty, thirty minutes at the most."

Longarm scratched his chin and took on the expression of a man lost in thought, then said, "You, by any chance, familiar with a retired lawdog living 'round these parts name of Amos Black?"

Wheeler's face lit up like a July Fourth whizz bang, then went a bit strange. "Oh, hell yes. Everybody in Amarillo knows Amos. Been livin' 'round these parts ever since folks first started calling this place Oneida. Ain't a finer feller as you'll ever meet."

"Glad to hear that."

"Oh, don't misunderstand, Marshal Long. Have to admit, he's a bit on the odd side. Might even say strange. Or maybe a better description is colorful. Yeah, colorful's the better word, but a fine feller."

"Colorful's not exactly what I expected."

"Yeah, well, have to see for yourself, I expect. Amos lives out on the mesa, bit west of the lake. Has a half-assed horse raisin' operation. Not much at raisin' horses, but then I don't think he tries real hard. His place is only a short piece on up the road from Mrs. Dawes's house. Sure she can point you in the right direction, or bet Old Mike can haul you out to Amos's digs, if'n you want."

Longarm nodded his appreciation, then headed off. He spotted the hack parked out front of the depot as soon as he turned the corner. An elderly man—who bore a striking resemblance to a woodcut rendering of the famed Buffalo Bill that Longarm had once seen in a Denver newspaper—crouched in the shade beside the front wheel of his buckboard. The bearded codger puffed on a hand-rolled smoke and scratched in the dirt with a long splinter of wood shaved from a pine picket lying at his feet.

Soon as the geezer caught sight of a potential paying customer, he hopped up and hobbled toward Longarm. "Give you a hand with yer gear, mister?" he said.

Custis Long waved the old man away and said, "Thanks, Mr. Turnipseed, but I've got it all seated in just the right spot. Only a few more steps to your rig, anyway."

Turnipseed's piercing, slate blue gaze never left the face of his newest client. As Longarm threw his load of paraphernalia into the freight box of the well-used buckboard, the distinguished-looking codger stood to one side and said, "We know each other from sommers, mister?"

Longarm grinned, then hefted himself up into the wobbly

wagon's passenger seat. "Name's Custis Long, Mike. Deputy U.S. Marshal Custis Long. Marshal Wheeler sent me your way. Said he figured that Old Mike Turnipseed would be more than happy to take me to Mrs. Dawes's roomin' house."

Turnipseed's face lit up with a broad, snaggle-toothed grin. "Ah. Well, you bet. Yessiree! And tell you what, Marshal Long, you don't have to call me Old Mike, 'lessen you want to, a course. See, there used to be a Young Mike, but he went and got hisself rudely kilt. Horse kicked him in the head 'bout a year ago."

"Damn. I'm right sorry to hear such sad news."

"Aw, he wuz always a problem child. Guess God just decided to come get him one day. Probably best for everybody all the way around. Way I saw it, the boy wuz destined for a bad end from the time his momma birthed him. Hell on wheels even as a small child. Turned into a man most folks didn't care to run across."

"I see. Well, then, Mike sounds fine to me."

"Good. Good. By any chance you that feller who got off the train with them juiced-up soldier boys what went to work a-killin' each other?"

Longarm nodded and grinned. "Yep. That'd be me alright."

With one gloved hand grasping the metal rail around the top of the buckboard's seat and the other resting on the front wheel, Turnipseed cocked his head to one side, then said, "Guess you musta seen that poor bastard get runned over by the damned ole train?"

Longarm pulled a fresh cheroot from his jacket pocket, shoved it into one corner of his mouth, and bit down but didn't light it. Between gritted teeth, he said, "That I did."

Turnipseed nodded as though he understood his passenger's unspoken thoughts, then clambered aboard and settled onto the unpadded board seat next to his fare. He snatched a long, thin buggy whip from its holder, then gently tapped the roan gelding harnessed to the rig. The horse strained forward, and the buckboard eased into a broad, dusty street that appeared to head north and west. Away from the depot, and away from the bloody scene of Trooper James Clyde Wadkins's brutal departure from what traveling evangelists liked to refer to as "this vale of tears."

Far as Longarm could tell, from what he could see as they passed the Turnipseed's wagon, Amarillo was a town locked in the bustling upheaval of being built. Framed but unfinished buildings and piles of unused lumber lined both sides of the rutted street. Noise from hammers, saws, and teams of struggling animals emanated from every direction. Busy workmen yelled to one another atop half-finished structures. Temporary signs identified some of the fragmentary buildings as the future sites of grocery or mercantile stores, law and land offices, liquor stores, meat markets, and drug stores. The only permanent structure in view appeared to be a U.S. Post Office where a spanking new flag flew from a shiny metal pole out front.

Longarm flicked a finger from one side of the street to the other. "Your Marshal Wheeler have his jail anywhere in the midst of all this tumult, Mike?"

"Naw. Bart mostly works out'n a tent down the street a piece. See that tree yonder?"

Longarm nodded.

"Only one still standin' within a quarter mile of the railroad, as you might note. Few 'tween here and Tascosa, but not many. Anyhow, the Marshal's tent's set up right beneath 'er. Drunks and them as violates local laws get shackled and chained to the tree. City fathers claim as how they're gonna build a jail soon as they can. Sure as hell need a decent lockup 'round here. 'Specially of a Saturday night. Does get rowdy on a Saturday night."

In pretty short order, Turnipseed's wagon approached a sizable canvas structure decorated with an elaborate, false store front. The good-sized joint sported a massive billboard over the entrance, lettered in bloodred. Sign identified the place as Tiger Jim's Saloon and Billiards Parlor. Window next to the entrance displayed a second notice. Hand-painted directly onto the beveled glass, it colorfully trumpeted the availability of the coldest beer in the Texas panhandle. Libation could be purchased for the paltry sum of a mere ten cents a glass.

Turnipseed elbowed his passenger, then grinned like a school kid and said, "How 'bout a snort a somethin' that'd make a grasshopper fight a curly wolf, Marshal Long? If'n you ain't in no hurry, we can stop. Have a nip or two. Know if'n I'd just seen a man get halved by the iron wheels of a passenger train, might want a beaker of panther sweat of some kind myself. Take the edge off'n everthang. Know what I mean?"

Longarm cast a travel-wearied glance at the entrance to the rugged, unfinished watering hole. Something deep inside the man told him in absolutely crystal clear terms that he shouldn't do it. He should go on to Mrs. Dawes's rooming house, then look up Amos Black as soon as he possibly could. In spite of such misgivings, he nodded, then pointed at one of the hitch rails out front of Tiger Jim's.

"Well, Mike, my friend," Longarm said, "when you're right, you're right. Feels as though I aged twenty years on that damned train. Then came the business with that soldier boy gettin' chopped in half. Suppose a swallow or two of something that bites back wouldn't hurt a bit. Be my pleasure to stand for a couple. Why don't you go on ahead and pull 'er up."

Chapter 6

The walkway in front of Tiger Jim's Saloon and Billiards Parlor was nothing more than a series of rugged, unframed boards laid out atop the bare, sandy ground. Some still sported long stretches of attached tree bark. The two-inch thick, warped, rough-cut timbers hadn't even been nailed down. They squirmed and flopped underfoot as the unlikely duo strode to the batwings and pushed their way inside.

Placed across a series of empty whiskey barrels, the cow-country watering hole's crude bar appeared to be constructed of the same substantial planks used for the boardwalk. The rugged cantina's platform for serving drinks started two or three steps inside the front door. It ran for fifteen feet along one of the heavy, canvas tent's sidewalls. Here and there, spittoons sprouted from the rude, dust-covered floor like oversized, shiny brass mushrooms. By way of something akin to a nod at decoration, a variety of moth-eaten stuffed animal heads hung from the canvas structure's center posts.

The back bar sported an enormous beveled mirror, four feet high and every inch of ten feet long. An elaborate slab of smoky, beveled glass dangled from a strand of thick wire draped over a square-headed, twenty-penny nail the size of a man's finger. The hand-formed spike was driven into a single four-by-eight of the wooden framework that held the tent's flopping canvas sides and roof erect.

Below the mirror, a sparkling array of amber and clear oddly shaped glass bottles clad in colorful labels lined a single piece of rough-cut timber exactly like the bar itself. A quartet of fully occupied poker tables took up most of the open space in front of the area for dispensing liquor. A couple of tired-looking, hard-eyed women moved from one poker table to the next as though walking underwater. A pair of spanking-new, felt-covered billiard tables took up almost all the available floor space in the back half of the tent saloon.

Several whiskey-weary types leaned on the far end of the bar. They watched as a quartet of dust-covered brush poppers sucked on mugs of cold beer and worked at shooting a game of snooker. One of the whiskey guzzlers at the bar glanced around at Turnipseed and Longarm as they entered, then elbowed a friend and nodded.

A rail-thin bartender in a sparkling white shirt, pasteboard collar, shamrock-colored garters on his sleeves, and a black vest hustled over just as Longarm and Turnipseed got settled. He slipped his thumbs into the vest's pockets as though to highlight the sparkling ropy gold chain across his belly.

"What can I do you gents for," the drink slinger said, then flashed the phoniest, most insincere smile Longarm had seen in years.

Turnipseed grinned like a possum in a pumpkin patch, then said, "Just gimme one a them cold beers. Colder the better, by God."

Longarm flipped hard money onto the bar. The five-dollar piece twirled, then fell to its side with the wonderfully ringing tinkle of real gold. "Rye. Best you've got. Maryland Gold Label would be nice, but I'll take whatever you have."

Their drinks had barely hit the splinter-laden wooden plank when the flushed, thick-necked lout at the end of the bar yelled out, "Hey. You there. Ain't you that feller what 'uz down there at the depot when that soldier boy fell under the train? Have anything to do with that? Reckon you mighta tipped his poor ass onto the tracks."

As though to himself, Longarm said, "Shoulda known. Hell's eternal fire, way this day's been going, I just shoulda known."

He clinked his glass against Mike Turnipseed's mug and tried his best to ignore the surly drunk. As surreptitiously as possible, he glanced up at the watery images in the mirror, sipped at the double shot of throat-stinging rye, then cut a squint-eyed glance toward the end of the bar.

The snarling bullyboy gave the top of the bar a resounding smack with one ham-sized fist, then snarled, "I'm talkin' at you, mister. You fuckin' deef, or somethin'." Then he turned to his bar mate. "Believe that, Alf? Son of a bitch is actin' like he don't fuckin' hear me. Goddamn, but they ain't nothin' can make me wanna bite the head off'n a horseshoe hammer like havin' a man ignore me when I'm a-talkin' at him."

Longarm watched every move from the corner of one eye as the belligerent jackass pushed away from his chosen spot near the billiard tables, staggered around to the front of the bar, then moved to a spot no more than five feet away. Legs spread in a hostile stance, half-empty bottle in one hand, the quarrelsome windbag swayed from side to side like a Red River cottonwood in a stiff breeze.

"You hear me talkin' at you, mister?" the bull-necked, bleary-eyed loudmouth growled. "Them big ole ears a yern chocked plum fulla horse shit or somethin'?"

A silence, like grinning death, seemed to have suddenly walked into Tiger Jim's joint and swept across the room. Poker players fell motionless and mute. Bets appeared as though suspended in midair. The rattle and click of falling chips faded into a tense stillness. Sounds of friendly laughter and convivial companionship vanished like morning dew on the Jornada del Muerto's bleakest stretch of sun-scorched sand.

Many of the taciturn risk takers folded their cards into neat stacks, then craned their necks in hushed anticipation of whatever entertaining butchery might be on the verge of transpiring. Several of the more prudent minded raked their piles of chips into slouch hats and heeled it for the door. It appeared to Longarm that those card benders who chose to stay on recognized the opportunity for some much needed amusement and weren't inclined to miss whatever was about to transpire—even if it held the distinct possibility of getting hit by a stray bullet themselves.

Longarm felt an invisible but palpable wave of animalistic expectation emanating from those who remained seated at the green felt tables behind him. He leaned toward Turnipseed and whispered, "You know this ignorant-assed, belligerent wretch, Mike?"

Turnipseed whispered back, "Yeah. Ever'body in town knows 'im. Think he's kicked hell outta damn near every adult male in these parts, one time or t'other. Whipped my skinny old ass year or so ago. Beat up on Young Mike a time or two. Still don't know exactly why he done the dance on my tired old ass, or what in the blue-eyed hell set him off. Near as anyone can tell, though, he's just one a them fellers what seems to go through life with his stinger out, constantly lookin' for an opportunity to put big angry bumps on the heads of all mankind."

"Truly?"

"Oh, yeah. *Absolutamente, mi amigo.* Name's Jimbo Duer. I'd be right careful with 'im, if'n I 'uz you, mister. He's meaner'n a sore-footed scorpion."

Jimbo Duer glared around the room as though looking for anyone or anything to redirect his hot-eyed attention. He slurped at his bottle again. A goodly amount of the amber-colored liquid dribbled down his chin and onto his necker-chief and the front of his already soaked and faded chambray shirt.

Longarm took another sip of his drink, then out of the corner of his mouth said, "Son of a bitch sure 'nuff has the look alright. Bully all the way to the bone." He gazed into the bottom of his glass, then motioned for the bartender to pour him another round. As the golden liquid gurgled from the bottle, he mumbled, "Damn but I do hate a bully, Mike. Just bein' within a hundred yards of one makes the hackles on the back of my neck stand up on end like porcupine quills."

Duer continued to glare around the room as though he expected someone to step forward and challenge him.

Turnipseed stared into his drink and tried to act totally unconcerned with Duer's presence. He fiddled with his mug, then said, "Well, you done found yerself a soulless ruffian and thumper of men. This 'un goes 'round just lookin' for somebody to stomp hell out of. Seems as how stompin' hell out of a poor unsuspectin' feller's his life's work. Well-known 'round these parts as one who'll jump on a body like ugly on a horned toad's ass, for no reason whatsoever. Usually kicks hell outta at least one or two fellers a week."

"One or two a week? You just tellin' me a stretcher, Mike?"

Longarm ignored Duer again when the swaggering bully yelped, "You listenin' to me, mister. Hear anything I've said, you ignert bastard."

Turnipseed shook his head, then whispered, "No. Swear 'fore Jesus, Marshal Long. Guess he must be low on this week's quota 'bout now. Even seen him whip hell out'n a woman or two my very own self. Usually happens when he cain't find a man to beat up on. Man's livin' proof they's more horse's asses than they is horses."

"Wonder what his gripe is with me?"

"Aw hell, you know his kind, Marshal. Ole Jimbo don't need no reason for his brand of viciousness. Don't have to have any gripe with a feller in order to kick his ass. He's jus' born cussed. Meaner'n hell with the hide off."

Longarm snickered. "Ugly, too. With a face like that, bet his momma had to feed him with a slingshot."

In spite of himself, Turnipseed snorted a surprised chuckle into his beer. He wiped foam off his face with a shirtsleeve, then said, "Well, he musta been down at the depot when that soldier boy bit the big one. Guess he seen you there. Don't matter, though. If'n it warn't that, he'd find another reason to come after you. Man's got somethin' up his craw with you a-ridin' on it, friend. 'Cause of what he seen, I guess. Then again, maybe not."

Duer swayed away from the bar, then moved two steps closer to Longarm and Turrnipseed. He threw down a sloppy swallow from the bottle in his hand, then said, "What the hell you two ole crones whisperin' 'bout? You ole women talkin' 'bout me?" He pointed at Turnipseed with the bottle, then added, "Best watch yersclf, ole man. Done seen to you once. Ain't no problem to do fer you again, just any time I please."

Then the menacing drunk took another step Longarm's direction before he finally stopped again. With his bulbous, vein-riddled nose damn near in Longarm's ear, he growled, "Answer me, goddammit. Talkin' 'bout me, you stringy sonofabitch?"

Tired to the bone, fed up after a long day's series of irritating and tragic events, Custis Long came off his elbows, rose to his full six-foot-four-inch height, then turned to face the sour-smelling Duer. He hooked a thumb over the buckle of his cartridge belt so his hand rested near the butt of his Frontier model Colt.

Longarm stared down into Duer's whiskey-blasted eyes and in a voice that even Turnipseed had trouble hearing said, "Look, friend, I'm wore slap out. Just arrived from Denver after a long, long, uncomfortable train ride. Not looking for any kind of trouble. Just want to enjoy my drink, then get a good night's rest. Why don't you go on back to watchin' your friends at the billiard table and leave us to our libations?"

Duer looked confused. "Libations? Libations? Oh, yer drinks." His lips peeled back to reveal a set of yellowed, tobacco-stained, decaying teeth. He glared up into Longarm's face and said, "I ain't your fuckin' friend, you fancy-talkin' stack of walkin' steer shit. And I don't care if you just got finished pumpin' a railroad handcart all the way from that Rocky Mountain rat hole established especially for pussies, while packs a injuns rode along pepperin' your ignert ass with poison-dipped arrows."

Longarm blinked back salty tears, then leaned away from Duer's rancid-smelling breath. A quick glance toward heaven for something like guidance seemed to incense the quarrelsome man even further.

"Pay attention, fart sniffer. Still ain't answered my question, goddammit. You pair of assholes talkin' 'bout me?"

A tired, knowing grin etched its way across Longarm's face. "Well," he said, "to be absolutely truthful, sir, we were just discussing the sorry lives of unrepentant fist fuckers. Now, if you consider yourself one of that elite group, then, yes, we were indirectly talking about you."

Duer's brain couldn't quite follow the joke and appeared

to seize up like an ungreased wagon wheel. His eyes crossed. He shook his head as though he'd been slapped. Appeared to Longarm as though one of the cogs in the man's thinker mechanism might have snapped.

Then, of a sudden, a scarlet wave oozed from beneath Duer's filthy collar and washed over his unshaven face. "Well, I'll jus' kiss my very own big, hairy ass. You callin' me a fist fucker, mister?" he hissed.

Longarm smiled again—a big, open, friendly smile. The kind of smile he knew would push a man like Duer to the absolute limit of his ability to deal with a set of circumstances of his own making.

The bully's eyes widened. He puffed his chest out, then slapped his bottle onto the bar. It wobbled in place and almost tipped over. He grabbed at the cuffs of his shirt and started rolling the sleeves up.

As though talking to a misbehaving youngster, Duer said, "I'm gonna whip you like a redheaded stepchild, you smart-mouthed sonofabitch. When I get through kickin' your ass, this stupid ole bastard standin' 'side you'll have trouble identifyin' what's left. Then, just for the fun of it, I might go on ahead an' kick his bony ass, too."

Still smiling and speaking so low Duer was forced to stop fiddling with his sleeves and twist his head sideways and lean forward to hear, Longarm said, "You'd best reconsider that threat, you stupid cocksucker. 'Cause you've got just about five seconds to get away from me. I've had one helluva sorry day so far. My head aches so bad I'd have to be dead three weeks before it'd stop hurting. Worse, you're well on the way to pushing me into just the kind of mood to stomp a ditch in your big stupid ass, then stomp it dry."

Duer snatched his bottle up, took a guzzling swallow, banged it back onto the bar, then ran a hairy arm across his whiskey-dripping chin. A good six inches shorter than Longarm, the quarrelsome drunk growled, "That a fuckin' fact, little man?" He tilted his head toward the friend who still stood at the end of the bar. "Here that, Alf? Do you goddamn believe it? This here cocky sonofabitch done went and threatened me."

"I heard 'im. Threatened you. Yessir. Sure 'nuff."

"Ain't a good idea to threaten a bucker'n a snorter like me, is it, Alf? Could get a man hurt so bad he'd have trouble walkin' or eatin' for months at a stretch."

Duer's friend fiddled with his drink, then flashed a weak smile. "No, Jimbo. Ain't no good idea a'tall to go an' threaten a feller like you. You're the biggest, baddest son of a bitch in all of north Tejas."

As surely as if he'd announced his intent through a carnival barker's megaphone, the arrogant, booze-saturated bully telegraphed his first blow by making a ham-fisted grab for the whiskey bottle he'd left sitting on the bar. He even managed to latch onto the long, glass neck, but the effort was slow and clumsy from beginning to end.

In a blur of controlled, concentrated action, Longarm's right hand snaked to the ivory grips of the pistol lying across his belly. Before Duer could get the bottom of the bottle off the bar, the heavy, five-and-a-half-inch steel barrel of the Colt Frontier model .45 came out of nowhere and landed against his temple. The pistol slammed against Duer's rock-hard noggin like a load of brick dropped from a second-floor construction job.

The sickening crack of metal against bone shot around the room. Men at every poker table flinched as though they'd personally taken the crushing blow. A long, ugly gash from one ear to the corner of his mouth opened as though Duer'd been sliced with a well-stropped razor.

As Amarillo's most famous ass kicker went down onto one knee like a poleaxed steer, Longarm's clenched left fist came around and caught the man with a thunderous, devastating lick flush against the jaw. Duer's head snapped sideways toward the bar. The mouthy drunk's skull smacked against the edge of the thick plank and bounced back.

Bottles atop the bar rattled in place and several fell over, rolled, dropped to the floor, and burst in a shower of sparkling shards. The glassy-eyed tough toppled sideways just in time for Longarm's pistol barrel to land against his already damaged face from the opposite direction. The stunned bully's hat flew off his head and dropped over the open mouth of a spittoon as though it had been carefully placed there by the owner. A fist-sized glob of blood along with half a dozen rotten teeth squirted from between Duer's flapping lips. The entire mess landed in a gooey puddle atop the booted foot of a gambling dude at the table nearest the action.

Horrified, the gussied-up dude couldn't take his eyes off the mess on the toe of his well-buffed boot. Of a sudden, he jumped to his feet and puked everything he'd had to eat that week onto the top of the poker table's green felt cover. His friends hopped up, swore, and headed as far away from the action as they could get while swatting flecks of his stomach contents off their vests and coats.

Duer dropped onto his back like a sackful of anvils thrown from the top platform of a West Texas windmill. For several seconds he flopped around like a beached catfish. Then, to the gaping crowd's total astonishment, the groggy bruiser rolled onto his hands and knees and actually tried to get back on his feet.

Beer in hand, Mike Turnipseed backed away from the bloody skirmish and moved all the way to the end of the bar nearest the batwing doors. He watched in horrified fascination as the friendly man he'd just picked up at the railroad depot holstered his silver-plated pistol, then kept his word by proceeding to stomp the living hell out of Jimbo Duer.

Duer coughed, crawled several feet, gagged, then spit another strangling gob of blood and teeth onto the floor beneath him. Somehow, he grabbed a table leg, pulled up onto his knees, and almost got himself into a standing position again. He had managed to move a few feet in the direction of his friends, when Longarm's booted foot went up, then came down between his shoulder blades. The staggering jolt that would have easily stunned a Percheron draft horse knocked Duer flat. He landed hard on his face. His head bounced off the floor like a kid's rubber ball. Spectators covered their eyes, turned away, and then groaned as once again Duer struggled to get onto his knees.

One gambler, who'd backed into a corner near an unused potbellied stove, said, "Jesus, why don't he stay down? The feller that's kickin' his big, dumb ass don't appear to be the least bit tired."

Longarm strode around in front of Amarillo's famed bully in residence, then kicked him in the chest. The booted blow sounded as though Duer's tormentor had stomped the top of an infantry troop's company drum to pieces. The drunken, beaten man hit the floor hard on his side, then slowly rolled onto his back. His chest heaved as he sucked in as much air as he could. Blood poured from the cuts on his face and the gaping holes where his rotting teeth and once resided.

"Stay down, you son of a bitch," Longarm hissed. "Stay down, or I swear to Christ, I won't leave enough of you for the bartender to sweep up on a dustpan."

Bleeding like a slaughterhouse steer, covered in all manner of splattered gore, puke, tears, and snot, Duer flopped around on his back for several seconds, then finally stopped moving altogether. Men huddled in the farthest corners of Tiger Jim's Saloon could hear his ragged, coarse breathing.

One of Duer's friends, a brush popper who wore an enormous, tall-crowned, Texas-style hat and stood near the billiard tables, shouted, "Don't get up, Jimbo. Don't get up, for the love of God. This feller'll kill you sure as a longhorn steer'll hook you in the gizzard." Then he shook his cue stick at Longarm and said, "Leave 'im alone, you vicious sonofabitch. Hell, you've hurt 'im so bad he ain't gonna be no more problem."

Hand on his pistol grip, Longarm whirled on Duer's friend and snarled, "Damned right he ain't gonna be no more problem. And soon's the evil wretch recovers enough to understand what just happened, you're gonna be the one to tell him what I did. And you're also gonna tell him that if I ever hear anything about him bullying anyone else or of him slapping some poor, defenseless woman around or if I so much as hear his name whispered around me again, I'll come from wherever I am—even if I'm somewhere on the other side of the world—and finish up on what I just started. You get all that, you mouthy bastard?"

The chastised brush popper nodded, then mumbled, "Yessir. Every word. I'll surely tell 'im everythang you just said. Swear on my sainted mother's memory."

Longarm twirled on his heel, then stomped his way to the batwings and back out onto the boardwalk, with Mike Turnipseed a few steps behind. Longarm jerked a cheroot from his pocket, fired it, thumped the still flaming lucifer into the street, then took several deep drags before he turned to the ancient hack driver and said, "Sorry 'bout all that, Mike. 'S not the kind of thing I'm inclined to do unless sorely provoked. Try my best not to get involved in such doings when at all possible."

Half-finished beer in a mug still in hand, Turnipseed nodded, then flashed a big grin. "Hell, I'd a paid good Yan-

70

kee money to see what you done to that evil snake. Sonof-abitch's had an ass whippin' comin' for as long as I've known him. If'n I hadn't been here to see it and somebody come up to me tomorrow and just told me 'bout how you whipped his butt, can't even imagine how much I'd regret not bein' here for the show. Yessiree, you just made my whole month. Maybe my entire year."

Longarm puffed at the stogie, shook his head, then stared at his feet for a second. "Can't say as how it gave me much pleasure to kick hell out of an idiot like him, though. Figure I'll probably wake up regrettin' the whole incident tomorrow mornin'."

"Well, wouldn't worry much 'bout feelin' all guilty over beatin' the shit outta ole Jimbo if'n I wuz you, mister. Think ever'body inside heard you try to get him to back down or leave you alone." Then the white-bearded gent reached over and patted Longarm on the shoulder. " 'Sides," he said, "bet if'n you took a poll of them as witnessed the dance, they'd all agree as how what you just done's been long overdue. Not kiddin' when I tell you that Duer has deserved an ass kickin' of the first magnitude for about as long as anyone 'round these parts can remember. Some a them boys inside might act like they's upset, but trust me, ever' one of 'em wuz hopin' you'd kill 'im deader'n the bottom of an open grave 'fore you went an' quit."

Longarm squinted, then stared off toward a boiling sun that sat in a cloudless sky two fingers above the horizon. "Yeah, well, tell you what, Mike, don't figure I'm fit company for women, church-goin' folk, or kids right now. Rather than stoppin' at Mrs. Dawes's place, how 'bout you take me on out to Amos Black's ranch. I firmly believe it'd be best if I spend the night there. 'Sides, it'll save me the trouble of having to run Amos down tomorrow."

Turnipseed nodded, then turned his mug up and drained the remaining liquid. After wiping his mouth on his sleeve, he said, "Whatever you'd like to do suits me right down to the ground, Marshal Long. Lemme put this here glass back on the bar, and we'll be on our way out to Amos's place. But let me give you some advice 'fore we start out. You'd best brace yourself for a bit of a surprise. Amos Black's something of an oddity, if you catch my drift. Colorful but odd."

Longarm puzzled for nearly an hour over Turnipseed's enigmatic observation about Billy Vail's old friend. By that time, the sun rested on the horizon like half an enormous, fiery ball sitting atop a table. Shadows had grown long and ominous. Here and there, coyotes yipped. Wolves skulked behind sandy hills and howled their love of the coming night.

The road out of Amarillo had quickly turned into nothing more than a pair of deep, dust-filled wheel ruts. Five miles or so away from civilization, Longarm's guide turned the rattling buckboard onto a rugged, barely discernible path that led almost due north along the banks of Wild Horse Lake. Leafy cottonwoods grew in some profusion east of the rough trace nearest the water. In the dying light, their moisture-deprived, wind-blasted, leafless cousins—west of the primitive trail—resembled tall, deformed, decaying tombstones.

Turnipseed drew his team to a halt near one of the ugly, scarred, twisted, rotting trunks. He cast a puzzled gaze at the wonders ahead, then said, "See what I mean, Marshal Long? Eerier'n hell, ain't it?"

In the diminishing glow offered by a dying sun, Longarm gazed in wonder at the peculiar display ahead. It appeared that every tree he could see exhibited some sort of strange decoration. Nearest the spot where Turnipseed had drawn to a stop, the gnarled corpse of a black jack oak sported an enormous, splintered board with the burned-in message:

PRIVATE PROPERTY
KEEP THE HELL OUT
STAY OFF'N MY ROAD.

Below that pointed notice, atop the tree's exposed roots, someone had stacked piles of bleached animal skulls of every kind, shape, and description. The pile of skeletal remains appeared at least three feet deep. Hung from a sizable branch of the same tree, a second sign cautioned the reader:

THEM AS TRESSPASS WILL BE SHOT AND
LEFT TO ROT.

Longarm sighed, then said, "Appears to me the man's serious 'bout his privacy, Mike. Real serious. Any chance he might go and shoot us 'fore we can get to him and explain why I'm here?"

Turnipseed snorted out a mocking chuckle, then slapped his animal's back with the reins. "Oh, he's serious alright, Marshal. Ain't many folks 'round here bold enough to challenge him either. But Amos knows my wagon—and me—and I don't think he'll shoot us."

"How much farther do we have to go?"

"Mile, maybe two. But, trust me, trip's gonna be interesting to say the least. Yep, if nothin' else, it's gonna be damned interestin'."

Chapter 7

The farther Longarm and Mike Turnipseed rolled down Amos Black's outlandish, coarse road, the more bizarre and eerie the wayside decorations became. The number and variety of phantasmagoric sights in either direction proved nigh on impossible to absorb. His strange displays became more fanciful and grotesque in the retreat of dying sunlight and the rapid rise of a monstrous, full, silver-tinted moon.

Here, the passerby could view the torched remainder of a covered wagon burned down to the wheel hubs—with what Longarm took to be charred mannequins laid out like the remains of dead bodies. There, near a bizarrely mis-shapen tree, a table and chairs were arranged in such a way as to make it appear ready for company to sit down for dinner.

Beneath an umbrella-shaped weeping willow, the limbs decorated with the shriveled, dangling corpses of dozens of small animals, stood an empty wooden washtub and a rub-board atop a hillock of shattered crockery shards. Nearby lay a small mountain of rusted coffeepots, piles of old shoes, mounds of what appeared to be moldy harnesses and ancient cavalry saddles. In another spot, several rolltop desks, a stack of ladder-back chairs, and rockers of various sizes and types ominously rose from the darkening landscape. The discarded detritus of those who'd traversed the area on their way to somewhere else simply added to the overall, skin-crawling creepiness of the place.

But while Black's bizarre exhibits of useless furniture, superfluous household items, and dead animals in various states of decay could easily give the softheaded a case of the wobbling willies, he compounded any passing viewer's feelings of discomfort with even weirder showings. With the power to make the hair stand up on a strong man's neck, other spots offered up spine-chilling displays of what Longarm took to be complete families of restored skeletal remains: dogs, cats, horses, cows, along with some animals impossible for him to identify, perhaps rabbits, skunks, wildcats, and such, or maybe an insane combination of several of those.

Some of the madcap presentations were surrounded by heaps of twisted limbs taken from outlandish trees only viewable to most people in feverish nightmares. And either near, above, or amidst each monstrous collection, another sign would always appear that warned of even more dire consequences for unwanted encroachment on the owner's gloriously peculiar property. All those menacing pronouncements were lettered in a paint colored exactly as one would suppose dried blood should appear.

Less than a minute before darkness draped itself over the entire earth like a funeral shroud, Turnipseed pulled his wagon to a halt out front of the most wickedly outlandish dwelling Longarm had ever seen in all his born days. The residence appeared as though constructed from foundation to rooftop of the same type of deformed, lurid timbers used on so many of the shocking exhibits they had passed. Altogether, the dwelling looked very much like a dynamited beaver's den that had been put back together by a crew of drunken carpenters.

Turnipseed leaned close to Longarm's ear and whispered, "See. If nothing else, you gotta admit the man's colorful. Even if you've never met him or never will. But, hey, this ain't the half of it. Wait'll you lock eyeballs on Amos. Now, that there's a sight to behold."

Those breathy, prophetic words had barely rolled off Turnipseed's tongue, when a voice from the inky darkness on the structure's east side called out, "You bastards illiterate? Cain't neither one of you read? My signs warn anybody comin' on this property of a direct, uncluttered path straight to a spot in a fiery hell. 'Pears as how you boys are lookin' for me to punch your tickets for the ride."

Longarm's fingers tickled the grips of his pistol as his companion said, "Come on now, Amos. You know me. Mike Turnipseed. Figure as how you've got me lined up in the sights of that big ole shotgun you favor, but you gotta hold up. Brought someone out here 'specially to palaver with you."

Several seconds of uncomfortable silence passed before the darkness spoke again. "I've told you before, Mike. You're not supposed to bring anybody out here. That means the sonofabitch with you right now. Don't want to see, talk with, socialize with, or otherwise mingle with anyone—anytime. Got that?"

"But, look Amos . . ."

"You heard what I said, goddammit. Now turn that wagon around and get on back to town."

"Billy Vail sent me," Longarm said. "He told me you were the kind of man who might be willing to help with a serious law enforcement problem."

Of a sudden, a man the casual observer might easily have mistaken for a grizzly on the prowl for food stepped from the shadows. His ill-kept mass of flowing hair hung down on broad shoulders. A beard the size of a gravedigger's shovel hid most of his face—except for deep-set eyes that seemed to disappear into his head like lumps of coal. Thick of chest and heavily muscled beneath a fringed leather jacket the size of small tent, he appeared in damned good shape for a man who had to be in his late sixties or maybe older.

"Where do you know Billy Vail from, mister?" Amos Black growled.

Longarm relaxed a bit and allowed his hand to move a few inches from the butt of his weapon. "He's my boss. Name's Custis Long, Mr. Black. Deputy U.S. Marshal Custis Long. These days Billy's the Chief U.S. Marshal workin' out of Denver. He sent me out here to catch a killer name of Simon Grimm. Grimm murdered a couple of Billy's other deputies near the town of Mesquite, down on the Palo Duro River. He figured if Grimm made a run for the canyon, I'd likely need the help of someone who could boast some familiarity with the area. Said you were the man."

Black lowered his long-barreled Greener and held it against one leg. With his free hand, he scratched his hair-covered chin, then his matted head. For several seconds, he swayed back and forth like an animal that couldn't decide the best path given the problem confronting it.

After nigh on a minute of scratching, grunting, and inde-cision, he waved a stubby-fingered paw at the two men in the wagon and said, "Well, shit. Might as well get on down. Come inside. We'll have a snort. Smoke some. Talk it over. See what comes to pass."

The interior of Amos Black's grotesque residence could not have come as a ruder shock. Its exquisitely furnished rooms looked exactly like what one would expect of the finest home in downtown Austin. Once Longarm got over the threshold, he could barely contain his profound surprise. It appeared as though Black had built as traditional a home as anyone could possibly imagine. Then he'd completely disguised the exterior, even the roof, with a disconcerting layer of the deformed, misshapen tree limbs and trunks he'd also placed in many of his perplexing, repellent exhibitions along the road.

Acting the part of gracious host, Black slid his big popper into the only empty space of a glass-fronted mahogany gun rack standing just inside the door. He motioned his guests to a spacious parlor off the foyer, thence to the comfort of overstuffed leather chairs typical of a wealthy ranch owner's den. He offered drinks and served his guests with all the grace and manners of a Southern cavalier prior to Mr. Lincoln's War of Northern Aggression.

When it appeared his visitors were finally comfortable, Black flopped into the largest seat in the room, swirled his half-filled glass under his nose, inhaled its essence, then said, "Well, get on with it. Why'd Billy Vail think I'd be of any assistance in the matter you mentioned?"

Longarm took a sip of the golden, sweet-smelling rye, then nodded his approval. "Can't answer that one, Mr. Black."

"Call me Amos. Never have been comfortable bein' Mr. Black. My grandpa was Mr. Black and everybody called Pap the Colonel."

"Well, Amos, all Billy said when he gave me this assignment was that if I needed a man familiar with the area in and around Palo Duro Canyon, I should contact you. Met Mike at the depot and he agreed to bring me here."

"Well, I've been there a time or two for sure, but I don't claim to be no expert. Even so, you have the idea that I can help with your manhunt. That it?"

"Way I've got it figured," Longarm said as he swirled the liquor around in his owl glass, "Simon Grimm's had plenty of time to run. Been more'n a couple a weeks—maybe as much as several months—since he arrived in the Palo Duro area, then murdered George Brackett and Junior Pelts. The canyon seems like the logical, closest place for him to hide, to me anyway. No matter how little or how much you've traveled there, it's more than I've done. 'Course, I could be wrong. Wouldn't be the first time."

"Damnation," Black muttered, then shook his head like an enormous old dog with a tick in its ear. "Say this bastard went and kilt Junior Pelts?"

Longarm grimaced, then nodded. "Afraid so."

"Shit. Knew Junior Pelts back when he and I 'uz just a couple a shirttail kids chasin' them damned bloodthirsty Comanche all over hell and yonder. Man was rougher'n a petrified corncob and tough as a razorback sow's snout. An' you're sayin' this Grimm feller managed to kill 'im?"

Longarm stared into the bottom of the glass and snapped a curt nod at Black. "Done both of 'em in with a double-bit ax."

A look of stunned disbelief flashed in Black's near ebony eyes. "Take your word on that, Marshal Long, but, well, that's damned hard to believe. Junior warn't the kind you could keep busy for half a day by havin' him look for the top of a pistol ball."

"You're right. I've worked with him a time or two in the past. One of the most competent of Billy's cadre of deputies. But Simon Grimm's a whole different kind of skunk. Man's murdered near a dozen people in the most hideous ways imaginable. Worse than the methods used by the Comanche at their most vicious."

"You know," Black said, and gazed at his flawlessly plastered ceiling, "once saw Junior take three arrows on one of our raids." He tapped various spots on his body, and added, "Got 'im in the right thigh. 'Nother 'n broke a rib—that 'n came nigh on to killin' 'im. Caught a third one in the upper back. Three weeks later, he went back out again and kilt ten a them savages all by his lonesome."

"No doubt about it, Junior was tougher'n the back wall of a shooting gallery. But, evidently, even cuttin' his teeth on a gun barrel didn't help against a beast like Grimm."

A vacant, distant quality crept into Black's voice when he said, "Guess not. God comes to get you, there just ain't no way to hide from 'im. Leastways, not any as I know of."

"True," Longarm said. "But there is something we can do to avenge the brutal departure from this earth of two good men. I can deputize you as part of my posse, and we can track Simon Grimm down. Drag his sorry ass to justice. If you could see your way to going with me on this raid, I'd appreciate the companionship, any advice you want to share with me along the trail, and your considerable expertise regarding the local geography."

Without hesitation, Black said, "When you wanna leave?"

"Tomorrow morning. We can catch the stage to Mesquite. Be there before noon."

Black grunted out something that sounded like, "Harrump, harrumph," then said, "no need to ride on that damned mud wagon the Lone Star Transport and Freight line calls a stagecoach. Be kinda like sittin' astride a fresh felled oak log with all the bark still on it. And you don't have to rent a horse. Got more'n enough animals right here for you to choose from. This is a horse ranch, you know. There are them as don't think so, but they're all milkin' the wrong cow. Absolutely certain we can find a comfortable ride for you in my stable that'll serve the purpose."

"One more thing," Longarm said.

"And what would that be?"

"Just wondered if you could put me up for the night?"

A surprised smile creaked across Black's face. Pearly whites glowed from behind his thick beard. "Oh, hell yes. Got plenty a space here. Four bedrooms. Pick whichever one strikes your fancy."

Longarm scratched his chin, then said, "What the hell does a man alone need with four bedrooms?"

Black cast a blank gaze around the room. A room that could have been transplanted from any plantation home in the South. "Had a wife when I started this project. We'd planned on a big family. But she died. Came down with pneumonia our second winter of marriage. That 'uz fifteen year ago. She's buried on the knoll out behind the house."

Appearing completely bushed, Mike Turnipseed had listened to the entire conversation without comment. When Black appeared overcome by painful memories, Mike said, "Reckon I could stay over, too, Amos? Not sure I care to make the trip back to town in the dark. Got a good moon and all, but I still don't like bein' out on your road of a night."

Black coughed out an odd, strained chuckle, sniffed, then rubbed his nose. "Hell, Mike, that's just the point, ain't it? All the work I've done over the years appears to have paid off in the exact way I hoped. Even my friends don't like to travel my road once it gets dark."

Sunup the following morning after a breakfast of eggs, fatback slab bacon, grits, and biscuits big enough to put an elephant in the shade, Longarm and Black loaded their gear onto a pair of fine animals and headed south for Mesquite. By the time they pulled out, Mike Turnipseed had already been nothing more than a dusty memory for near an hour. Said he had to get back to the depot and the prospect of some passenger business as soon as possible. He shook

Longarm's hand, threw Black a friendly nod, and rattled away.

Longarm picked a long-legged, line-backed dun for the trip. Given the comfortable seat he'd chosen, the cloudy day, the heat abating a bit, and Amos Black's amiable companionship, the more than thirty-mile ride went by without a hitch. Nothing seemed amiss until they arrived atop a gentle rise covered in big bluestem grass a mile or so outside Mesquite.

As the men rested their mounts, Longarm pulled out a nickel cheroot and stoked it to life. He flicked the still smoldering lucifer away and stared down at the colorful spot of businesses, homes, and greenery that lay hard by the Palo Duro River.

"Nice lookin' little town from up here," he said.

"Mesquite's that for sure," Black said. "Only town its size as I know of in these parts what can boast a brick-covered main thoroughfare."

"Be damned. That pissant lookin' place's main street is bricked over?"

"Yep. 'Course the entire avenue ain't much more'n two or three hundred feet long. Not but two dozen or so businesses on the whole street. Yeah, folks what established the place had great hopes for the future. Me, I think she'll be history in a few years. Just ain't much a nothin' out this way. Man's gotta be lookin' for a pissant-sized burg like Mesquite to find it."

Of a sudden, the unnerving sensation of icy fingers running up and down Longarm's spine hit him like a sledgehammer. It was the kind of inexplicable sensation that had served him well for years. The sense that someone or something was watching or lying in wait with malicious intent. He shivered, squirmed in the saddle, then stood in his stirrups and shot a quick, uneasy glance over his shoulder at their back trail. Nothing there. He scanned the horizon in every direction, then snatched another quick peek over his shoulder again. Not even a blade of grass out of place. Nothing he could detect. Or perhaps the threat really was there, and he just couldn't see it.

Chapter 8

Marshal Talbot Butterworth motioned for his visitors to sit, then trundled his well-fed bulk around a banker's heavy oak desk. The blubbery lawman flopped into a thickly padded matching office chair. He grabbed the wooden arms of his squeaking throne and rocked back. The much-abused seat beneath the Mesquite city lawman's substantial caboose squawked its displeasure at being so rudely abused. Even the most casual observer would have agreed that Talbot Butterworth looked irritated and more than a bit uncomfortable over the appearance of strangers who'd dared to invade his office kingdom. His personality definitely reminded Longarm of Billy Vail's testy clerk, Henry.

With some amusement, Longarm watched as Butterworth gave the imposing Amos Black the kind of eyeballing usually reserved for something as freakishly bizarre as the Tasmanian Wildman. The Wildman was, supposedly, a hair-covered whim of nature that traveled about the Texas countryside with a two-wagon carnival. Longarm had run across the itinerant act more than once in his vast travels. He figured the nomadic carnies probably visited Butterworth's remote village at least once a year—around pig-killing time.

Butterworth's round, glowing, baby-ass pink face finally broke into a strained, counterfeit grin. "What can I do for you fellers?" he said.

Longarm leaned forward and pushed his bona fides and deputy U.S. marshal's badge over.

Butterworth glanced at the badge, but made no effort to read any of the carefully arranged sheaf of letters, warrants, official documents, and such. He snatched up the leather wallet containing the star-shaped symbol of Longarm's authority, then gave it—and the federal lawdog's identification papers—a quick, judgmental look. Of a sudden, his entire demeanor appeared to change. With considerably more care, Mesquite's lawman placed the leather badge folder onto his guest's pile of documents, then slid the entire package back across the desk.

Something akin to a look of genuine relief washed across the stout city lawdog's face. "Hot damn. Marshal Long, is it?" Butterworth said.

Longarm nodded.

"Well, Marshal Long, must admit, I'm happier'n a three-tailed puppy you fellers have finally arrived. Gotta say, though—and please don't take any offense at my bluntness—it's about fuckin' time. Was beginning to think your immediate superiors might just be pulling my big, fat, hairy leg with telegrams from Denver sayin' someone 'uz on the way out here to investigate this sow's nest."

Longarm retrieved the meticulously organized wad of documents, shoved them into his jacket pocket, then said, "I can assure you, Marshal Butterworth, we got here as fast as we possibly could. I'm confident you must certainly recognize that time and distance do have a way of slowing our response to any particular situation—even one as urgent as the brutal murders of two of our fellow officers and friends."

Butterworth waved a meaty hand as though shooing a

nuisance fly away. "Aw hell, Marshal Long, please call me Tall. Everyone else does. Been callin' me that since I 'uz a kid."

He sounded more than a bit puzzled when Longarm said, "Tall?"

Amos Black made an odd, strangled sound, then covered his grinning mouth with one hand.

Butterworth's pink face flushed scarlet. "Yeah. Tall. Name's Talbot. But my younger brother couldn't get his mouth around the word. Started callin' me Tall when we 'uz kids. Name stuck. Now everybody, and all their relatives from outta town, calls me that."

Amos Black flashed a toothy, mischievous grin from behind his thick beard. "From the look of you, Butterworth, *Round* mighta been a better choice of monikers," he said.

Longarm thought sure Mesquite's thickset lawman would react poorly to Amos's lame effort at humor. He was surprised when the corpulent city marshal threw his head back, let out a hearty guffaw, and slapped the arm of his chair. Then he pinched at the roll of fat around his ample middle and said, "Pretty obvious as how I don't spend a whole lotta time pushin' myself away from the dinner table, ain't it—hell, any kind a table what's got food on it for that matter. Wife says if'n I don't give my right arm a rest, real soon like, I'm gonna be as big as a melon-shaped boarding-house cat."

Butterworth's effort at self-deprecation went miles toward breaking the feeling of icy distance that had existed among the men only a few seconds earlier. As their comfortable chuckles faded, he said, "Guess I should back up a bit. Say as how I truly am pleased to meet you. Murders of them friends a yours have put me in a state of near personal panic since the day I found their remains."

"Certain it's not much fun when you have to pick up the

mortal remains of the badly butchered bodies of men who've been chopped into several pieces like nothing more than sticks of firewood," Longarm said.

"True," Butterworth said, "very true. But, hell, fellers, findin' 'em chopped up don't come nowhere close to the worst of it. No, sir. Nowheres close."

Longarm shot a quick, puzzled glance at Amos Black, then looked back to Butterworth. "Not sure, exactly, what you mean by that, Tall. Marshal Billy Vail gave me the impression Grimm's ax work on George and Junior was the bottom line worst of it. Surpasses all my ability to understand how much more awful their deaths could have been than that."

Butterworth's piggish gaze flicked back and forth from Longarm to Amos Black. "Got not the slightest idea what Marshal Vail told you boys, but my telegraph messages to him about the situation out here couldn't have been any plainer. Made it my mission to describe the state of affairs exactly as it exists to this very minute."

The distinct feeling that he was chasing his own tail swept over Longarm. "Perhaps you should explain exactly what we're talkin' about here, Marshal Butterworth. Have to admit, I'm beginning to feel kinda like the woodpecker that found itself in a petrified forest. Sounds like I might've missed something when I spoke with Marshal Vail."

Butterworth drummed nervous fingers on the top of his desk, ran one back and forth in a dusty spot, then wiped the powdery residue on his shirt. "Grimm done somethin' awful to them boys he kilt, Marshal Long."

"Awful? What's that mean? How much more awful than getting chopped to pieces with a double-bit ax can this tale be?"

"He done somethin' so awful I still have trouble believin' it." Butterworth appeared to lose his train of thought and began to mumble. "Yeah, truth's still right difficult to stomach. Even though Doc Strange confirmed in no uncertain terms exactly what I'd originally thought from the get go."

Longarm shifted in his seat. "Why don't you just go on ahead and spit it out, Tall? Think that's the best way to handle whatever you've got on your mind."

Beads of sweat turned into small rivers that ran from the hefty marshal's crinkled forehead. He leaned over on both elbows, slanted an arched-browed glance around his office, then spoke in a husky low voice as though he didn't really want to be heard. "Son of a bitch not only kilt them poor fellers, by choppin' 'em up, Marshal Long, hell's jinglin' bells, he ate some of 'em, too."

Butterworth's breathy assertion dropped on the sheriff's office like a bolt of heaven-sent, electric blue, pitchfork lightning. A clap of thunder violent enough to knock the building off its yard-thick foundation could not have had more stunning results on his shocked visitors.

Longarm jammed a finger in one ear, then swirled it around as though trying to scratch a spot on his brain. He pushed up in the chair, then glanced at the finger like he'd somehow found the offending remark Butterworth let loose. A look of flabbergasted surprise on his face, he coughed into his hand, then said, "Not sure I heard you right, Tall. Did you just say Simon Grimm ate George Brackett and Junior Pelts? Ate some of 'em? That is what I heard, wasn't it?"

Grave-faced, Butterworth nodded.

Amos Black let out a pained groan. He slumped over with his elbows on his knees. "Sweet sufferin' Jesus, Marshal Long. You didn't say nothin' 'bout us goin' out after no fuckin' cannibal."

"Good God Almighty, Amos, I didn't know anything about Grimm bein' a cannibal myself till just now. You heard the same thing I did, at the exact same time. Billy Vail didn't say a single, solitary word to me about cannibalism. You sure about this, Tall? There ain't no doubt in your local pill popper's assessment?"

"Seemed pretty sure 'bout it all when me'n Doc Strange talked it over after I brung what was left of them poor boys back to town. He found saw and knife marks on the bones, human teeth imprints in some of the flesh we give 'im, and such. Said the evidence was clear as a glass dinner bell, far as he was concerned."

Black groaned again, then said, "You mean there was chewed on parts of them poor men left?"

Butterworth looked painfully uncomfortable. "'Course," he barely whispered. "Sorry bastard couldn't eat all of 'em. Just pieces. Parts. Select cuts, as it were. Leastways, that's as near as me'n Doc Strange could tell."

Black looked stricken. "Jesus, save us," he muttered.

Longarm tried to lock onto Butterworth's nervous, darting gaze but couldn't. "You sure it was Simon Grimm did the deed, Tall, not some animal that happed on the corpses?"

"Hell, yes, it was Grimm. I knew the man. Helped him find that shack he was livin' in, few miles on down the river. Didn't know who he really was at the time, of course. Told me and claimed as much with everyone else he met when he came into town that his name was Elton Peevy. Said his sainted wife and family of seven children perished in a house fire somewheres over in the Green River country of Utah Territory. Guess he'd been livin' here for nigh on six months when them two deputy marshals showed up."

Longarm scratched his jaw, then squirmed in his seat. "So George and Junior came by here and talked with you before they went out to Grimm's cabin?"

Butterworth stared at the top of his desk and, of a sudden, appeared to look guilty. "Yeah. Sure. Them boys had

90

wanted dodgers with woodcut renderin's of Grimm on 'em. Hell, I knew exactly who they 'uz looking for soon as I seen 'em. Even offered to go out to his place with 'em and help round 'im up. They said it'd be best if I hung back, let them take him down, 'cause of him being so dangerous and all. They claimed as how the man was such a threat to life and limb that they didn't feel comfortable involving me or any of the local folk hereabouts in the arrest."

"You didn't go out with 'em?" Amos Black said.

"No. Hell, no. Did exactly what I 'uz told. But then them federal boys left and never come back. Waited three days. On the mornin' of the fourth 'un, figured it best to stroll on out to Grimm's cabin for a look-see myself." A trembling hand shot up to Butterworth's sweat-drenched brow. "My God, but it was the closest thing I've ever experienced to walkin' into a slaughterhouse. Body parts strung out all over hell and yonder. Some pieces of 'em poor bastards was in the fire. Hangin' on hooks. Even found parts still sittin' in tin plates atop the table in the cabin. Jesus, I come on bones what appeared to have been gnawed on. Looked like an unfinished meal. Scared the hell outta me right then and there, that's for damned sure."

"What'd you do?" Longarm said.

"Did what I think any reasonable person would've. Jumped on that hammerhead a mine and fogged it back to town quick as I could. Got Doc Strange. We slipped back to the cabin, real carefullike. Gathered up ever'thang we could find what looked like a body part. Doc put most of 'em fellers back together. Almost looked kinda like real bodies when he finished. Almost, but not quite."

Amos Black sounded stunned and distant when he said, "Put 'em back together?"

"Well, yeah. 'Course they wuz parts what had gone

missin'. Not a helluva lot, mind you, but some fairly important parts anyway."

Longarm grimaced, then said, "Gone missin'? Like what?"

"Both heads. Never did find them boys' heads. A hand or two. And pretty much all of an individual haunch of'n each corpse. Figured as how Grimm must a had a real taste for human haunch meat—the left one in particular—for some odd-assed reason. Maybe the crazy bastard thinks that 'uns not as stringy, more tender, or somethin'. Doc said the whole mess sure as the devil looked like a classic case of cannibalism to him."

"Holy Mother of God," Black groaned.

In a moment of stunning clarity, Longarm said, "Does anyone else here in Mesquite know about this?"

With an emphatic shake of the head, Butterworth said, "Oh, hell, no. My momma didn't raise no idiots, Marshal Long. I mean, can you imagine the kinda panic we'd a had around these parts if'n I had formed up a posse, stormed out there, and ripped around like some kinda certified loon. Think I'd let this story get out? Nope, I didn't tell nobody. Me'n Doc buried what 'uz left of them poor bastards quick as we could. Even done the interment at midnight so's no one would see. Gave me the creepin' willies, tell you for damned sure. Swore Doc Strange to secrecy. Didn't even tell my wife or Whip."

"Who's Whip?" Longarm said.

"Jonathan Whippet Cannon, my deputy. Everyone calls him Whip."

"How on earth did you know what you found was the remains of them two deputy U.S. marshals?" Black said.

Butterworth's face twisted as though a gut-wrenching pain had hit him. "Well, hate to say it, gents, but that was the easiest part of the whole nightmare, really. Found clothing, wallets, badges, personal effects—all that kinda thing. Grimm left that stuff strewed all over the yard and inside that shack he called a house. Them boys' belongin's was lyin' around everywhere you looked. If'n you've ever been unlucky enough to come upon a Injun massacre, well, that's kinda like what I found. Couldn't a been anyone else but them two unfortunate deputy marshals. 'S why I sent to Denver for help."

"How can you be so sure?" Black said.

"Ain't nobody from right here in Mesquite that's gone missing. 'Course, Grimm coulda took some poor soul out in the wild places as I don't know about. But, hell, I ran across animals what belonged to your friends on my second trip out with Doc. That Brackett feller rode a right handsome paint pony. Couldn't help but notice that colorful hay burner when he rode away from my office the day the two of 'em came by askin' after Grimm. Found that horse wanderin' around not far from the shack. Still saddled and ever'thang. What me'n Doc Strange managed to scrape up was your compatriots alright, Marshal Long. And that's the ugly facts of the situation."

An uncomfortable silence washed over the room. The banjo clock on the wall behind Butterworth's desk seemed to grow louder with each mechanical second it ticked off.

Near a minute passed. Longarm wagged his head back and forth, then said, "You have any idea where Grimm headed when he left? Billy Vail seemed to think the murderous skunk might have beat a hot path straight for Palo Duro Canyon."

Butterworth nodded. " 'Pears that way to me, and that's exactly what I told Marshal Vail in my telegraph message."

" 'S damned remote, ain't it? Not much out that way."

"Remote's a good word to describe the place, that's for damned sure. Know if I 'uz on the scout runnin' from the law, remote's what I'd damn sure be lookin' for. Hell, Comanche and lots a other Indians hid there for thousands a years 'fore anybody even knew the place existed."

Longarm nodded. "I've heard it's rougher'n a petrified corncob out thcre, Marshal."

Butterworth grinned. "Six hundred feet deep in places. More'n a hundred miles long. Bleak but beautiful. No lack of water, though. Prairie Dog Town Fork of the Red River runs right through it. Lotta nooks, crannies, caves, and such to hide yourself in—that's for certain sure. Damned few people to bother you—some but not that many. Body could go for days and not see another livin' soul."

"But there are people living in the canyon?"

"Oh, sure. Dozens of folks just tryin' to stay away from civilization. They're scattered here and there. Scratchin' out a living raising a few cows and horses."

"That it?"

"No. Ole Charlie Goodnight's got people running cattle down in there as well. But, hell, you could go for weeks and not run across any a them boys. No doubt about it, Palo Duro Canyon's a great place to hide from the law, Marshal Long."

"My deputy, Amos, here, is somewhat familiar with the spot. Sure we'll do just fine."

"That's all well and good, but I gotta be truthful with you fellers. I don't envy you goin' out there after Grimm, not one little bit. He could be hidin' behind any rock, hoodoo, or bush along the way. Kill you quicker'n double-geared lightnin'. 'S why I ain't been out there after the murderin' skunk. Nope, don't envy you boys scratchin' 'round after him in the canyon, not one little bit."

Chapter 9

Longarm stepped from Marshal Talbot Butterworth's office, then stopped beneath the shade-giving portico that covered the jail's front door. He leaned against one of the porch pillars, lit a cheroot, and gave Mesquite's main thoroughfare a leisurely going-over.

Amos Black eased up to Longarm's side and said, "Don't know 'bout you, Long, but I could use a drink. Great time a day for a glass of panther sweat. One 'bout as potent as liquid gunpowder might do the trick. Then again, hot as it is out here, even though the sun's on its way down, a glass of cold beer might be even better."

"Take it you didn't care for what Marshal Butterworth had to tell us in there just now."

Black snatched off a hat the size of a midget's washtub, then wiped his sweat-covered forehead with a blue bandanna. As he swabbed out the hat's soaked interior leather band, he said, "You just about take it right. Have to admit, there's somethin' 'bout sittin' 'round chewin' the fat over the possibility of folks cookin' and eatin' each other that makes my mouth drier'n the heart of a South Texas haystack."

Longarm squinted and pointed around the street with his

smoking cigar. "See at least three saloons from where we're standin', Amos. Just pick whichever joint you fancy. I'll be more'n happy to stand for a couple of cold ones. Maybe sit around and take our ease till it cools off a bit out here."

Black jumped at the offer. "Top Hat's a damned good spot. Know the feller what owns the joint. Claims to serve the coldest beer 'tween here and Tascosa. Personally, I think he's right."

"What about the Bale of Hay 'cross the street yonder? Kinda like the name of the joint. And it's closer than the Top Hat. Hell, you can almost spit on the place from here."

"Trust me, Marshal Long, Top Hat's a much nicer joint," Black said, then jammed his hat back on. "And my friend don't water his liquor or beer like that snakey bastard who owns the Bale of Hay."

Longarm shrugged, stepped off the boardwalk, and pulled his animal's reins loose from the hitch rail. He ambled down the middle of Mesquite's fancy, bricked Main Street with Amos Black in tow. Along the way, Longarm took note of the various businesses and shops on either side of the amazingly clean short piece of paved roadway.

It appeared, to the observant deputy U.S. marshal, that those astute businessmen who'd staked out a spot closest to the river provided potential customers with the fanciest, most colorful exterior facades. The Mesquite Bank and Trust, Mervin Popper, President—according to a brass sign on the building's most prominent corner—sported crystal-clear, beveled, leaded-glass windows. From the street, any passerby could observe the entire inside of the building and watch as customers conducted their business. Additionally, the imposing structure appeared to be the only edifice along the entire thoroughfare constructed of the same burned red bricks that matched those used to pave the street.

As the pair of lawmen planted booted feet on the shiny brass foot rail and bellied up to the Top Hat Saloon's mahogany bar, Longarm cut a sly, professional glance around the room. Place came nigh on to being completely empty. Of the five felt-covered poker tables along the wall across the room, only two had customers sitting at them. Three men lounged at one table pitching cards and money back and forth. One man sat alone.

It appeared the faro dealer and roulette operators had given up on any possibility of play that day. Both men loafed behind their games on padded wooden stools and nodded as though about to fall asleep. A bird cage and six dice stood idle atop the bar a few feet from where Longarm leaned on one elbow. And in the farthest corner, a brilliantly colorful wheel of fortune appeared dust-covered from neglect and lack of use.

Like a massive glob of cooking grease atop a red-hot stove, the liquor locker's fat-gutted bartender oozed over to his newest customers. With all the enthusiasm of a man who looked like he had an axle dragging in the dirt, the drink slinger said, "What'll it be, gents?" Then, displaying absolutely no pleasure for the task, he wiped at a spot on the bar with a piece of stained, wet rag.

Amos Black flashed a big smile, then said, "Beer. Colder the better."

"Make it two of 'em," Longarm added.

"Where's Shorty Pine?" Black said.

As he pulled on the spigot handle to draw their mugs of amber-colored beer, the bartender grunted, "Ain't here."

Amos grabbed one of the frosty beakers that came sliding down the bar, then said, "Well, shit, I can see he ain't here. Where'n the hell is he?"

As though bored beyond tears, the drink slinger grunted, "Gone to Tascosa."

Black slurped at his drink, sucked suds off his lips, then wiped his mouth on his sleeve. "Tascosa. What the hell'd he go to Tascosa for?"

The bartender gazed at the back of one hand as though suddenly interested in the pattern of the veins beneath the taut skin and nothing else in the world. "Had business up that direction. Leastways, that's what he said when he struck out yesterday mornin'. Think he might be tryin' to figure out how to move this operation up thataways. Sure as hell ain't nothin' goin' on here. Almost like prayer time."

"Got any quieter around here, think I could hear my hair growin'," Longarm noted, then grinned.

"Mesquite's gone and turned into a monumental bust, boys," the bardog grumped. "Town ain't gonna be long for this world if things keep on a-going the way they are right now. Hell, just look around. I've got six customers. You two and them four stingy-assed moochers scattered around at them tables over yonder. My opinion, we shoulda closed the doors two hours ago. Place belonged to me, I'd a already shut this sucker down."

Amos took a long drag on his drink, then twisted at the waist. With a wreath of beer suds clinging to his moustache and shaggy beard, he looked like a gargantuan hydrophobic dog. He said, "Hell, I know that ole boy yonder, Long. That's Petey Baxter. Man knows Palo Duro Canyon like the back of his hand, Long. Ole desert rat's been guidin' folks in and outta the place ever since the time Colonel McKenzie and the cavalry kicked the Comanches and Kiowas out back in '74."

Black's acquaintance, who bore all the outward appearances of a man totally engrossed in his drinking, was a study in hideous facial scars, gray hair, a single steel blue eye, and sweat-stained leather. A faded, wide-brimmed felt hat of indecipherable color decorated the back of a head that looked as big as the prize pumpkin at a harvest fair in October. A Sharps rifle stood propped against the table nearest the man's right hand. The ivory-clad grips of a bowie knife, with a blade that bore a striking resemblance to a meat cleaver, jutted from behind a leather bandolier strapped across his thick chest. A sweat-soaked leather patch that appeared to sink into the empty space behind it covered the vacant spot where his missing left eye had once resided.

Longarm watched as, with the beer in his paw, Amos Black strode to Baxter's table. The men shook hands. They exchanged pleasantries for about half a minute, then Black motioned for Longarm to come over and sit.

"This here's my good friend Petey Baxter, Marshal Long. Ole Petey, here, knows more 'bout Palo Duro Canyon than I ever will," Black said as they slid into two of the three empty chairs at the table.

Baxter shot a squinty, single-orbed, wary glace at Longarm as though he'd just discovered a tumblebug on his shirtsleeve. He nodded, but made no offer to shake hands. Longarm took no personal offense at the rough-looking scoundrel's lack of social niceties. Man's probably just not very convivial till you get to know him, he thought.

Billy Vail's favorite deputy marshal studied the man as the pair of old friends continued to swap good-natured small talk. From all appearances, Petey Baxter's sizable ass had been rooted to the chair for most of that entire day. The man's remaining eye was so shot through with red veins, he looked as though he was right on the verge of bleeding slap to death. A nigh on empty whiskey bottle sat on the table. The tumbler near the old ruffian's filthy right hand was filled to the rim and had overflowed onto the table's green felt cover.

For several minutes, Black and Baxter talked of everything in general and nothing in particular. But the tenor of their friendly discussion changed dramatically when Long-arm's new posse man casually mentioned that they would be on their way into Palo Duro Canyon the following morning.

Baxter snatched his glass up and threw the entire contents down his throat in one gulp. He slapped the empty container back onto the table top, then quickly poured another. He nervously twirled his refreshed drink around in the wet spot. From beneath the wild-haired, scar-split brow over his good eye, he shot nervous glances at his new tablemates.

In a hoarse whisper, Baxter said, "Somethin' strange goin' on out in the canyon, boys. Somethin' real strange. Right creepylike, if'n you ask me."

"Strange, Petey? Creepy? How so?" Black said.

Baxter gazed over his shoulder, then cast a worried look around the room and thence into every viewable corner. "Not sure, exactly, Amos. But there's somebody or somethang out there a-prowlin' 'round that's spooked everyone I've run across for the past couple a weeks."

Longarm leaned into the conversation. "Anybody you know who's seen whatever it is that's got everyone's balbriggans in a lumped up knot, Petey?"

Baxter shook his disheveled head. "Spite of what the superstitious and downright stupid might think, fer as I'm concerned, it's a man for certain sure. Seen some a his sign myself. Ran into a couple a cowboys from ole Charlie Goodnight's spread almost three weeks ago. They 'uz jumpier'n a pair a big ole fat-legged bullfrogs in a fryin' pan. Said they'd run across several slaughtered steers that day. Tole me that whoever or whatever kilt them animals done a nigh on to professional job a butcherin' the beasts."

Several seconds of tense silence passed before Amos said, "Them boys have any opinion on who or what *exactly* mighta killed their livestock?"

Baxter tilted his head back and glared down an oft broken nose with his one good eye. "Oh, hell, there's all kinds a idiot opinions flyin' 'round. Fieriest rumor has it that some Comanches done snuck off'n their reservation over in the Nations. Come back to the canyon lookin' fer some bloody payback fer bein' jerked off'n their land by the cavalry back in '74."

"Aw, hell, Petey, that's just a gigantic crock of bullshit, and you know it. Poor injuns is so beat down they ain't never gonna be any problem again," Black growled.

Baxter pushed back in his chair. "Could be. Could be. But people do talk. Yessiree, they do talk. But all I done said ain't the worst of it."

Black tilted his massive head, squinted, and growled, "Well, what then?"

Petey Baxter knifed another pointed glance over one shoulder, threw down another shot of panther sweat, and hissed, "Hear tell as how one a them cowboys disappeared t'other day. Way I heard the tale, he just up and vanished like a puff a smoke. Story goin' 'round is that some a his friends come on his horse all covered in blood, gore, and such. But they ain't never found him yet. Talked to one feller who was really spooked. Said they'd been hearin' some kinda weird, cacklin' laughter of a night. Gives me the pimply fleshed willies just thinkin' 'bout it, boys."

Longarm drummed his fingers on the table top. "Marshal Butterworth didn't say anything about disappearing cowhands."

"Doubt anyone's tole him 'bout it yet. Just happened, you see. They's still prowlin' 'round out there a-lookin' fer 'im. 'Sides, what the hell would Butterworth do even if'n he did know 'bout some poor missin' cow chaser. Tryin' to get that man to do anythin' 'sides sit on his sizable ass is like tryin' to talk Chinese to a armadiller."

101

Longarm mumbled something unintelligible but offered no real opinion on a subject he knew so little about.

Petey shook a finger at both men, then said, "You know me, Amos, ain't scared a nothin' I can see. But I tell you what, fellers, for more'n a week now I done kept gettin' the itchy-necked feeling a something or somebody was doggin' my trail. Watchin' me. Got me a-sweatin' bullets jus' thinkin' 'bout who or what it might be. Then t'other night, I heard that strange laughin' sound myself. 'S why I'm sittin' in the Top Hat a-suckin' on this bottle. Figure I'm a damned sight safer in here than wanderin' around out in the fuckin' canyon alone."

Petey Baxter's last word had barely dropped from his chapped, twisted lips when the Top Hat's batwing doors burst open and slammed against the wall. Longarm twisted around in his seat to see what the noise was all about. He watched as a stunning woman took two steps into the establishment, stopped, then laid a cocked, short-barreled Greener across one arm.

Tall, thin, and angular, the striking female was stringier than a strip of chewed rawhide. She had dressed herself in a split-crotched leather riding skirt and a skintight chambray blouse that highlighted perky, upturned breasts. Her broad-brimmed, Mexican palm-leaf hat was pushed to the back of her head. The sombrero was molded in a stylish crimp popular with Easterners who fancied themselves Texas cowhands. As she swiveled her head from side to side and gazed around the room, wheat-colored hair dropped from beneath the straw hat and tumbled onto squared shoulders.

Knee-high, stacked-heel riding boots with gold eagles stitched across their stovepipe fronts sported a set of solid silver spurs decorated with matching rowels the size of a man's fist. A faint, wondrously musical jingle followed her slightest move. The entire package was finished off with a brace of ivory-gripped Colt pistols strapped high on her narrow waist, the butts turned forward in the Wild Bill Hickok fashion.

As Longarm stared wide-eyed and open-mouthed, the tight-lipped gal took another step farther into the room. Then once again she drew to a halt. From the corner of his mouth he whispered, "If she's as good with those pistols as she is at wearin' 'em, must be hell on wheels in a gunfight, boys."

"Looking for someone," the woman called out. "Any of you lazy bastards Simon Grimm?" She scanned the stunned faces of the Top Hat's idlers. Waited a few seconds for an answer. When none came, she added, "Well, then, if any of you indolent, time-wastin' sons of bitches happen to know Simon Grimm, step on out and speak up. I'm willing to pay good Yankee gold to anyone who can direct me to the stink-spraying polecat."

Longarm jerked as though he'd been hit in the chest. He grinned, then shot a quick glance at the other men in the saloon. It appeared as though every gambler, drunk, and itinerant risk taker in the place had suddenly been struck by lightning.

Amos Black poked Longarm on the shoulder with a finger the size of the handle on a ball-peen hammer, then hissed, "Sweet Jesus, did you hear what that gal just said?"

"Hell, yes, I heard it. Not deaf yet. Just havin' trouble believin' my own ears is all."

One of the card benders two tables farther down shouted, "Hell, darlin', you can call me Simon Grimm if'n you'll come over here and sit on my face till I smother from the pleasure." His friends hooted and banged on their table's felt-covered top with closed fists.

The woman grimaced and shook her head. Then, from between gritted teeth, she called back, "Ugly as you are, mister, I wouldn't sit on your face if it was shaped like a silk pillow and stuffed with goose down."

Longarm's grin turned into a toothy, uncontrollable smile. He twisted in his seat and watched as the smart-ass's buddies slapped him on the back and encouraged him to continue with the verbal sparring. Evidently, the red-faced churnhead decided he was way overmatched and kept his stupid mouth shut. Longarm swung his gaze back toward the door just in time to see the dazzling female heading his direction like she owned the place and everybody in it.

The determined gal jingled up to within one or two steps of the table, then said, "You gents appear a bit smarter than that trio of booze-swilling, bunkhouse rats yonder. Figure you might not have clearly heard what I said. Either of you familiar with an evil stack of hammered manure named Simon Grimm?"

"Why thankee, ma'am," Petey Baxter said, winked at her with his only eye, then threw down another shot of coffin paint. "Glad you recognize a gentleman like myself when you sees one." He pointed at each of his tablemates. "Kinda company I have to keep these days makes it a mite hard fer a damned fine woman like yerself to tell that I'm a man of superior breedin' and upstandin' demeanor." About a second passed, then he burst into a fit of table-pounding laughter.

Longarm eased out of his chair, snatched his hat off, and held it over his heart. He ran a finger back and forth beneath his handlebar moustache, then said, "Pay no attention to our companion, ma'am. He's had a bit more than usual to drink today. My name is Custis Long. Deputy U.S. Marshal Custis Long as a matter of pure fact. And, truth is, I know exactly who Simon Grimm is." He pulled the only empty chair away from the table, then waved her toward it with his hat. "Wonder if you might like to sit a spell. We can discuss the man at length, if that's your pleasure."

Chapter 10

Several tense seconds ticked away. The woman eyeballed Longarm as though examining a nuisance bug she'd pinned to the bottom of the drawer where she kept her laciest, most private unmentionables. Then she flicked a surly glance at the other men at his table and appeared on the verge of walking away.

When her cobalt gaze locked onto Longarm again, he bowed slightly. Then, in his most ingratiating, Southern cavalier manner, he said, "Let me assure you, miss, you'll be quite safe at the table with me and these *gentlemen*. And, who knows, could well turn out that the three of us might be of some assistance in your search for the infamous Simon Grimm."

Finally, the stern-faced girl let the hammers down on her fancy, gold-inlaid, short-barreled blaster. An audible sigh of relief popped out of Amos Black. Petey Baxter rolled his only eye heavenward as though offering up thanks for a benevolent deity's grace.

"Alright," the woman said, then slipped into the chair Longarm offered. She draped the shotgun across her lap, kept her hand on the weapon's grip, and gazed up at him.

"But if this conversation takes any kind of lascivious side trip, I'll be out of this chair and back through those swinging doors faster than you can fire that fancy, cross-draw pistol on your hip, Marshal Long."

Longarm dropped his hat onto the table, then carefully eased back into his own seat. "You already know my name, miss. Gent on my right is Amos Black. Across the table there is none other than the locally famous Mr. Petey Baxter. Now, how 'bout tellin' us who you are."

"Rebecca McCabe," she said matter-of-factly, then nodded to each man in turn. Her voice took on a decidedly harder edge when she zeroed back in on Longarm and added, "I'm here for one reason and one reason only, Marshal Long—to kill Simon Grimm. I will not be deterred by any badge-carrying lawdog. All you have to do is point me in the right direction, then get out of my way. I'll send Grimm to Satan so quick, he'll be roastin' in hell faster'n small town gossip can travel through a church social."

Longarm fiddled with his drink and said, "And why on earth would a young woman like you say such a thing?" He slouched in his chair. A grimace etched its way across his weathered, handsome face. He twisted a pointy end of his moustache, then added, "You have any idea the kind of man you're so casually talkin' 'bout killin', Miss McCabe?"

Rebecca McCabe didn't miss a beat. She leaned forward, shook a finger in Longarm's face, and growled, "Know exactly what kind of man I'm out to kill, Marshal Long. That monster murdered my sister, her husband, and all their children in the Green River country over in Utah Territory."

Surprised by the stunning information, Longarm sat up, then said, "Terribly sorry for your loss, Miss McCabe. I'm well aware of those murders."

"Oh, you are, are you? Well, then, are you also aware that Grimm did the infamous deed in the most horrific way any upstanding Christian of good character could ever conjure up in their worst nightmares? And, perhaps as bad as the murders, that the law has let the lunatic get away from 'em a number of times already. I'm gonna find his sorry ass and make damned sure he never kills another soul the way he did my sister and her kids."

"You're a hard woman," Amos Black said. "Good lookin', but harder'n a bag fulla tenpenny nails."

A slight smile crinkled the corners of Rebecca McCabe's lips. "Tougher'n a boiled boot heel, Mister Black. Cut my teeth on the barrels of this big popper laying across my lap. Weapon belonged to my father. I intend to use it to send that fiend Simon Grimm on his slide into Beelzebub's sulfurous pit."

"While I sympathize and applaud your devotion to your family, Grimm recently killed two deputy U.S. marshals. If my count is correct, that'd make ten benighted souls he's sent to God," Longarm said. "I sincerely believe you'd be better served by letting men like us handle this situation."

Rebecca McCabe leaned toward Longarm again with a look on her face indicating she might just slap him so hard his eyeballs would spin in his head like a kid's top. "Now listen, Marshal Long. Listen very carefully. I've been on Grimm's trail now for months and am not about to let up or let you discourage me from carrying out my declared mission. A terrible undertaking I swore to complete before God over my brutally butchered sister's grave."

Longarm tried to match the McCabe woman's hard-eyed gaze. He soon found himself staring at his hands as her personal tale of murder and insanity unfolded before he could stop her.

"Tracked him from the Green River country to Cortez, Colorado, where he'd murdered and mutilated a man and wife name of Harrison. From there his blood-soaked trail led to Cuervo, in New Mexico Territory. Along the way he left four more bodies by the wayside. Know of at least three other deaths in Texas before I got here. And now, you tell me he's murdered a pair of deputy U.S. marshals. Seems to me you *professional* man hunters and law enforcement types haven't done worth a damn at stoppin' what might be on the way to goin' down as the most infamous murder spree in the history of the West."

"Still and all, Miss McCabe, I think you should leave the matter to me and my friend Amos. We'll be going out after Grimm tomorrow morning. Trust me, he won't get away to kill anyone else this time."

Of a sudden, Rebecca McCabe's glass blue eyes lit up with unchecked interest. "You know where Grimm is, Marshal Long?"

"We have a fair idea of his whereabouts."

"Then I'll go along with you."

"No. No. Don't think so, Miss McCabe. Not sure I'd want to take on the responsibility for your safety."

"I'd be more comfortable if you'd call me Rebecca, Marshal Long."

"Well, Rebecca, I . . ."

The McCabe woman leaned back in her chair. She stroked the stock of the shotgun as though it were a living thing. The strain of maintaining control over hidden emotions manifested itself in a single, pearl-shaped, crystalline tear that slid down her flushed cheek and dangled from a jaw set like case-hardened steel.

Her voice sounded like a dull saw going through oak knots or a cornered wildcat from the back of her den when she said, "I saw what this monster did to my sister and her kids, Marshal Long. Helped pick up their butchered bodies. Placed them in their coffins and helped bury them. Stood over my sister's grave and swore bloody retribution."

"I understand, Rebecca, but . . ."

"No. No, you don't understand. No way that you could. Not even by a country mile. As God is my witness, with or without your help, I'll find Simon Grimm. Use my father's shotgun, here, to cut him off at the knees. And while he still lives, I intend to amputate his manhood, stuff it in his mouth, then set him afire. With the good Lord's guidance, that's how this dance will all eventually play out. And there's nothing you could move in heaven or here on earth to change my determination in the matter."

Longarm ran a hand through his hair. "Wish I could truthfully say I understand how you *feel*, but must admit I can't. Not sure anyone could. And despite the kind of heartrending grievance that should assure you a place in our posse, I simply cannot agree to let you come along."

The corners of Rebecca McCabe's cobalt eyes crinkled. A slight, knowing smile played across her full, inviting lips. "Might as well get your mind right on the subject, Marshal Long. I'll be going with you in the morning. You can't stop me. And if you try, you just might find out it's a damn sight harder than you think."

"Aw, hell, Long, let 'er come with us," Amos said. "She's entitled. Hell, if anybody's entitled, it's this lady. I'll keep an eye on 'er. Grimm'll have to kill me to get to her."

Petey Baxter suddenly swayed to life in his chair and grunted, "Hell, I'll even go back out there with you boys. Not sure I really wanna go, but if'n this lady's got grit 'nuff to track a murderin' bastard like this Grimm feller all the way from the Green River country, least I can do is help her find 'im and kill 'im. Yes, by God, that's what I'll do fer damned sure."

Longarm rubbed one temple as though trying to extract some kind of burrowing irritant from his skull. "Alright. Alright. 'Pears as how I'm being outvoted here. But I'll be watching you as well, Rebecca. And if you can't keep up or turn into a problem or lose your nerve or go on a crying jag or whatever, I'll send you back to town so fast it'll set your garters on fire."

The McCabe woman pushed her chair away from the table and stood. She leaned into Longarm's face and hissed, "Do you really believe I could've made it from Utah Territory to a one-dog town like Mesquite, Texas, alone, if I was some kind of candy-assed little girl. You won't have to worry 'bout me, Marshal Long. You boys best be worried for your own safety. If and when we find Simon Grimm, I can take care of myself. Don't you doubt it for a second." Then she turned on her heel and headed for the street.

As Rebecca McCabe reached for the Top Hat's swinging doors, Longarm called out, "Where will you be tonight, Miss McCabe? Just in case I need to get in touch with you."

She stared over the batwings and motioned toward the east end of town. "Noticed a hotel down on the end of Mesquite's main and only thoroughfare. Figure to take a room there for the night. Don't worry, Marshal Long, I'm an early riser. Be an hour ahead of you, whenever you're ready to hit the trail tomorrow."

The yahoo gambler at the far table called out, "Need any company there, darlin'? Be my pleasure to ride along with ya, wherever yer bound. Keep your bedroll warm at night for ya. Always did like long, lanky women like you." His friends snorted, giggled, and pounded the table again.

Rebecca McCabe slowly turned her head just enough to cast a hot-eyed glare in the smart mouth's direction. "You come anywhere near me tonight, mister, and the local undertaker will bury you tomorrow." And with that she pushed through the batwings and vanished into the afternoon's rapidly dying glow.

"Where you boys gonna put up for the night?" Longarm said.

Petey Baxter waved a hand in front of his damaged face like he was swatting nuisance flies, then struggled from his chair. He weaved back and forth like a cottonwood in a cyclone, then steadied himself and said, "Hell, 's been so long since I slept in a bed, Marshal Long, not sure I could anymore—even if'n I wanted to. Make me a camp out behind the hotel and take my ease on the ground. More at home that way. Been sleeping 'side my mule for nigh on twenty years. No need to make any changes this late in the game. Meet you out front of the Mercury. Be ready to pull out at first light."

Longarm looked puzzled. "Mercury? Where's that?"

Amos pushed away from the table. "Name of the hotel that gal's gonna put up at for the night. Mercury Hotel. Right on the east end a town. Gotta head out that direction in the mornin' anyway. Might as well all meet up there. Probably the easiest thing to do. Figure I'll just put it down with Petey. Ain't all that fond of hotels myself."

Longarm stood, drained the last few drops from his beer, then wiped his mouth with the back of one hand. "Well, I don't harbor no prejudices against hotel beds myself. Think it'd be kinda nice to sleep on feathers for the last night 'fore we head on down into the canyon. May be a spell before any of us have a choice in the matter. So I'll mosey on down to the Mercury and take a room. Meet you out front with the lady at first light. Can you boys take care of my animal?"

Black and his one-eyed friend nodded and grunted their approval. "Oh, hell, yes," Black said. "Go on and chase after that gal, Long. Know that's what you have in mind. Actually, cain't say as how I blame you much. She's a looker alright. Damn near got a woody myself jus' a-lookin' at 'er."

Longarm strode to the batwings, placed one hand atop the café doors, and thoughtfully gazed after Rebecca McCabe's swaying figure as it gradually faded into the twilight. "I have to agree, Amos. She's a fine-lookin' example of womanhood. Bit rangy for my particular taste. The kind you boys in this part of the country really go for, though. A looker nonetheless. Have to be nigh on blind not to see it. But, you know, I'm not sure she'd be receptive to much in the way of advances from any man right now. Figure if I'd seen what she has, pretty sure I wouldn't want much to do with any of the hairy-legged variety for a spell."

Once outside, Longarm stopped at the hitch rail long enough to retrieve his possibles bag, shotgun, rifle, and bedroll. The disappearance of the sun had brought the temperature down considerably. The cool of the evening made a stroll in the moonlight right comfortable.

The desk clerk at the Mercury Hotel came as something of a surprise. The wispy blonde immediately reminded Longarm of Minnie Clay. Not that the two women looked all that much alike, but the straw-colored hair and turquoise eyes were enough to throw his mind into a lecherous, spinning memory of Cora Fisher and her aggressively sensual friend.

Didn't take much in the way of brain power to recognize the desk clerk's type as well. She could have had the label "Bored Country Girl" written on her forehead like a billboard. He knew without even thinking twice that the gal was easily impressed with any passing, near handsome, mysterious stranger.

Soon as Longarm stepped up to the desk, he caught the girl in a sideways examination of everything she could lay an eye on about him. Her gaze stopped on his crotch as she suppressed a lecherous smile. This is gonna be easier than catching fish with dynamite, Longarm thought to himself.

As he inked his name into the hotel's register, the curious clerk brazenly gazed at his upside-down signature and read aloud, "Mr. Custis Long, Deputy U.S. Marshal, Denver, Colorado." She twirled the book around and studied the signature as though to be sure of her initial notions. "How intriguing," she said, and flashed a fetching smile.

Longarm grinned back, tipped his hat, and said, "Correct in every detail, Miss. But you now have me at something of a disadvantage. What might your name be?"

A scarlet blush shot from beneath the clerk's frilly collar and darkened her cheeks. "Amanda. Amanda Calvert, sir. My father owns this establishment."

Taken by the girl's scrubbed, flaxen-haired good looks, and her all too obvious wide-eyed appraisal of his appearance, Longarm removed his hat, leaned onto the desk, and took her by the hand. "Guess that goes a long way toward explaining why a beauty like you gets stuck in Nowhere, Texas, at the registration desk. Tell me, beautiful Amanda, does your father ever let you get away from this desk, or does he keep you chained back there all the time?"

The fact that a man of the world had taken an interest in Amanda Calvert pleased the girl no end. Longarm could see all the outward signs of curiosity in the way the girl gazed into his eyes and squeezed the hand holding hers. "I ain't chained to this desk," she declared. "Come and go as I please. 'Sides, my father's out of town for the next several days. Won't be back for almost a week."

"Well, now, is that a fact?"

"Yes, it is."

Longarm leaned as far over the desk top as he could and placed his lips near the girl's ear. "Well, think you'd be interested in coming by my room later for a sip of rye and a little conversation?"

"Maybe. Maybe I would. What kinda rye?"

"Gold Label Maryland. Best money can buy. 'Course you might not be old enough for such grown-up pleasures."

She turned her head Longarm's direction ever so slightly and into his ear whispered, "You'd be surprised what a girl my age knows and does, Marshal Long."

"And what age is that? Just for the record."

"Nineteen. Had my birthday last month. Be twenty on the next one."

"That a fact?"

"Indeed. So I'll thank you not to think of me as a child. Given the opportunity, bet I could show a gentleman of the world, like you, a thing or two."

"Could you now? Well, then, why don't you stroll on up to my room a little later? Like I said, we can have a drink and then maybe you can demonstrate this extensive knowledge of worldly things of yours for me."

Amanda Calvert flashed a big-eyed, coquettish smile. She twirled a lock of golden hair around one finger, then whispered, "Everything pretty much dies 'round here by nine o'clock. Why don't you just get that drink ready and look for me a little after nine?"

Longarm pulled her hand up and kissed the palm. He thought for a second she might go straight into a babbling swoon. No doubt in his mind, the small-town gal had never, or at least rarely, been on the receiving end of so much exotic attention.

"Nine. Look for you then, beautiful Amanda." He started for the staircase leading to the rooms, but stopped and said, "Oh, by the way, in what room did you put the lady who came in just ahead of me?"

"She's right next door. You're in 204. She's in 203." The magnetic smile appeared again, but this time more mischief came through when she said, "Think she'd like to join us later, Marshal?" Longarm couldn't believe his ears. Perhaps Minnie Clay and Amanda Calvert were distantly related somehow. Didn't matter. Appeared an interesting evening had just fallen into his waiting, eager lap.

Chapter 11

Relaxed, buck-assed naked, and enjoying the ear-tingling buzz from three glasses of his favorite alcohol-laced beverage, Longarm lay propped up on two pillows wedged against his room's brass bedstead. Another sip of Gold Label Maryland rye washed over his tongue like velvet, then carved a fiery path down his expectant throat. The sound of a discreet knock—more like a scratching at his door—proved barely discernible over the humming in his head.

He rolled to one side and flicked a quick glance at his genuine Ingersoll railroad pocket watch. The turnip-sized, ticking timepiece was soldered to the opposite end of a thick, ropelike solid gold chain that connected it to his hidden .44-caliber, twin-barreled derringer. Watch, pistol, and gold connector rested near a flickering coal-oil lamp atop a small table near the head of his bed.

"Nine-oh-one," he muttered to the empty room. "Damn, but Little Miss Amanda Calvert sure as hell don't waste no time, does she? Come on in, darlin'," he called out. "Door's not locked."

The Mercury Hotel's grinning, impish, desk clerk pushed the thick slab of oak open and darted through the tiny gap she had allowed herself. Without a sound, she silently closed the entry, then leaned against it. "I ain't wearin' no underthings," she said, bit her knuckle, and giggled. "Took everything off, 'cept this ole dress, right after we talked earlier this afternoon."

Longarm's gaze locked onto the hand she slowly brought up to one breast. He watched as the smirking gal ran twitching fingers across her jiggling boob, then tweaked an already stiff nipple beneath the flimsy material. "Been pretty much nekkid ever since. Goin' nekkid 'neath my dress just makes me hotter'n the business end of a brandin' iron. See you musta done the same. You know the difference 'tween nude, naked, and nekkid, Marshal Long?"

"Hadn't given it much thought, Miss Amanda."

"Well, *nude* and *naked* both mean without clothes. *Nekkid* means naked and up to somethin' *nasty*. Are you up to somethin' *nasty*, Marshal Long?"

Longarm flipped away the sheet draped across his middle. His rampant dingus sprang toward the ceiling like the main mast on an English man-of-war.

Amanda Calvert's breath caught in her throat. Turquoise-colored eyes widened. Her hand dropped from her breast to the junction between her shapely thighs. While giving herself a vigorous rubbing, she gasped, "Good Lord A'mighty, Marshal. Ain't never seen one o' them thangs that big before. Heard tell of 'em. Never seen one. My feller's ain't nowheres near the size of that beast. My goodness, he's got a tiny little pecker compared to that 'un. Is it real?"

Longarm patted a spot on the bed. "Why don't you bring your pretty little self on over here and find out?" he said.

As quiet as a snowflake landing on a feather-stuffed mattress, one hand still jammed between her legs, Amanda barefooted her way across the floor. She dropped onto the bed and grabbed his rampant dong with the fingers of her free hand. She surprised him a bit when she abandoned her juicy cooze and snatched the glass from his fingers. In one gulp, the half glass of rye disappeared down the randy girl's eager throat.

She handed the empty beaker back, wiped her lips on the back of her hand, then said, "Guess you know as how my daddy'll kill the hell outta both a us, if'n he ever finds out 'bout this."

Longarm grinned, uncorked the gold-labeled bottle retrieved from a spot next to his watch, and poured more rye into the empty glass. "That a fact," he said. "Should I take it that your daddy is a very strict man?"

"Oh, yes, indeed. Pap believes that if you spare the rod, you'll most certainly spoil the child," she said, then leaned over, ran her tongue around the inflamed tip of his love muscle, and drew as much of it into her mouth as she could. Her lips came away with a loud, sucking smack.

She appeared entranced by his enormous tool and didn't take her eyes off the beast when she said, "But, lordy, lordy, I can't seem to help myself, Marshal Long. Just love to drink whiskey and do what daddy calls 'the nasty.' See, 'bout twice a week I get this buzzin' kinda hummin' itch 'twixt my legs. Almost drives me wilder'n a caged cat, if'n I cain't get something inside there to rub that buzzin' away. Must spend half my wakin' hours with my hand buried up to the wrist down there. Jus' be mixin' biscuits or washin' dishes or jus' anything a'tall, and 'fore I know it, I'm goin' at myself like somethin' tetched in the head. Know what I mean?"

With that, she jumped off the bed, grabbed the hem of her cotton dress, and, like a Mexican toreador twirling his cape during a Monterrey bullfight, whipped it over her head. Full, upturned breasts with heavy, blood-engorged nipples barely jiggled as she hopped up and down and giggled like a small child. The dewy triangle of hair between her legs glittered with jewel-like droplets of moisture left over from the clawing she'd just given it.

She pushed one breast up far enough so she could spend a second sucking herself. "You know," she said when her greedy lips popped off the now rigid nipple, "I started doin' the nasty when I was eleven years old. Did my cousin and a couple a his friends in a haystack out back a my daddy's barn." She swayed from side to side and hugged herself. "Boy, back then that 'uz 'bout as much fun as I could stand. Get to thinkin' 'bout that day 'fore I know it. Don't mean to. Just seems to pop up. So to speak."

"You don't have to tell me any of that, darlin'," Long-arm said, sipped at his glass again, then ran his free hand up and down his steely rod.

Amanda's overheated gaze locked onto his caressing fingers and said, "I like talkin' 'bout it. Like talkin' 'bout doin' the nasty almost as much as I like doin' it. And that's sayin' a mouthful. 'Course, there ain't many men I can talk with, like this, 'bout how I feel. See, way I figure it, you'll be gone tomorrow mornin', and we'll never see each other again, so it don't matter."

Of a sudden, Amanda leapt onto the bed with both feet. Spraddle-legged, she stood over Longarm, grabbed his railroad spike of a dong with both hands, then proceeded to slide herself onto it. About halfway down, the girl's gushing cooch tightened around him, then squirted so hard she almost blew herself away from the action.

"God A'mighty," she yelped, and tried her best to see what was happening between her own legs. "Ain't never come this quick before. Can't wait to get all the way to the bottom a this big ole thang a yours. Gonna ride you like a West Texas leather pounder tryin' to break the wildest cayuse in the corral."

Less than a second later, in the flickering, reddish yellow glow of the lamplight, Longarm watched Amanda's aquamarine eyes roll into the back of her head. As if hit by a pitchfork bolt of heaven-rending lightning, she took in the massive totality of his prong and then, suddenly, appeared to go slap crazy. With hands pressed against his heaving chest, her hair flew from side to side as she bucked and snorted. Her nostrils flared like a red-eyed, jug-headed hay burner bent on killing itself with pure, unbridled pleasure. Every other plunge downward resulted in a thunderous, fluttering gush from the slick, interior depths of her nigh on volcanic snatch.

After a crazed ride of near half an hour, she hopped off Longarm's rock-hard tool like a rabbit that had been hit with a red-hot branding iron. Gal came to rest sitting on his face. She grabbed the brass bedstead, smooshed her juice-filled quim against his overheated tongue, and yelped, "Lick it, lick it, lick it. Oh, yeah. That's it. Right there. Right there. God A'mighty, your tongue must be almost as long as your dick. Oh yeah, that's the spot. That's the fuckin' spot. Oh sweet Jesus, you're good!"

About the time he thought he might never breathe again, she stood, squirmed down his chest, unceremoniously dropped onto his stiff root again, and went back to bouncing on him like a thing insane. When Longarm thought she'd about worn herself to the proverbial frazzle, the huffing girl abruptly got to her feet again, twirled around, and slid down his pole with her back to him.

"Oh God, oh God, oh God. Big sucker's rubbin' a different spot now," she squealed. "Feels so good. That's it. That's it. Push up. Push up. Oh God."

Longarm let the sex-starved Amanda have her head for almost an hour, then, finally—tired and ready for some sleep—he took control of the situation for the gooey, juicy push to an ending. He grabbed the girl by the shoulders. Pulled her backward onto the bed. Then crawled between her flailing legs and slid into her waiting snatch with an ease that should not have but surprised him a bit.

Using his clenched, muscular, pile-driving ass to its maximum sexual efficiency, he single-mindedly drove into Amanda's gushing glory hole like a man possessed. The violent crash of their bodies slapping against each other sounded like pistol shots.

To his complete surprise and pleasure, Longarm discovered that the ardent Amanda absolutely loved to be ridden with her legs draped over his shoulders—a neat trick, considering the girl was near a foot shorter than her energetic lover. More surprising still was that with an ever so slight craning of the neck, the acrobatic position gave the flushed, sweating girl close to a perfect view of the action between her legs. During the entire ride, right up to the final thunderous, mutual climax, the energetic gal's hot-eyed, heavy-lidded gaze never left her slick, juicy, steaming notch.

Afterward, with one arm draped over the cooing Amanda's girlish waist and completely done in, Longarm drifted into a deep, sound slumber. But a restful night's sleep quickly crept away from him on bloody, clawed feet.

He tossed and squirmed and at some point pleasant, satisfying dreams turned into ugly skin-prickling nightmares. Perhaps the change was caused by a bit too much liquor. Or maybe his own neck had somehow got twisted the wrong way on the pillow. It could have easily occurred that he rolled onto his stomach and came near smothering in the bedclothes.

Whatever the reason, during that tortured night's attempt

124

at much-needed rest, Longarm's quiescent eyes squinted open on a scene of bizarre strangeness somewhere in the deepest realms of his dark, rarely explored subconscious. Amidst roiling clouds of fog and smoky mist, he saw himself riding through a barren, hellish, bloodred landscape astride a pale, skeletal horse. Dagger-shaped flames shot from the beast's mouth and eyes. And the rattle and click of the animal's bleached bones sent waves of icy goose bumps up and down his slumbering, sweat-chilled spine.

A relentless feeling of being pursued by an invisible, pitiless enemy swept through Longarm's entire dormant being. An agonized sense of helplessness caused him to toss and turn in the coils of his sheets. When the first rays of sunlight knifed across the heavens, he snapped awake. Sat bolt upright atop a mass of twisted, sweat-drenched bedclothes.

He quickly ascertained the passionate Amanda had abandoned him to the dark demons who tortured his fitful nap. In her place, a hastily scribbled not on the bedside table reminded him of her father's possible return. As he read the crude missive, he wondered where the girl had managed to find a pencil and scrap of paper.

After a flurry of concentrated activity, Longarm thumped down the narrow stairs of the Mercury Hotel, two at a time, then headed for the front entrance and the rugged inn's covered veranda. Loaded down with guns and other essentials, he swept past an unmanned front desk, through the lobby, and onto the light-poor covered entrance's rough-cut board porch.

Dawn's dim, grayish yellow light barely revealed Amos Black and Petey Baxter. A few steps into the street, near the edge of a pool of weak, coal-oil lamplight that flowed from the hotel's curtainless windows, the coarse-looking pair sat on animals that anxiously stamped iron-shod feet and switched their tails. Amos, one leg draped around the saddle horn, held the reins of Longarm's empty-saddled gut twister. From all outward appearances, Petey looked as though he was still asleep.

Off to one side, leaning against a convenient hitch rail, an impatient Rebecca McCabe slapped her mount's braided reins against a gloved palm and toed at the dirt beneath her feet. Even in the thin, poor light of coming dawn, Longarm detected dark circles beneath the woman's eyes. "We're burnin' daylight, Long," she said, then flashed a tight grin. "That's correct, isn't it? Burnin' daylight? Heard some cowboys in Rita Blanca, New Mexico, say that years ago when my family first moved to Utah Territory from the East. Always thought sayin' it like that made me sound like a real Westerner."

"Yeah," Longarm grunted back, "must be all of about twenty minutes after five." He knifed a tired glance at the rapidly brightening eastern sky, then snorted, "But, to tell the absolute truth, Miss McCabe, if there's enough daylight out here to burn, I sure as hell can't see it. Not yet anyway."

Rebecca McCabe's smile widened as she turned, then jumped into a waiting stirrup, stood, and eased one leg over her ebony-colored animal's back. She leaned slightly, snatched her shotgun from its fancy, hand-embossed scabbard, and laid it across the saddle's pommel. Longarm could have sworn he saw an arched eyebrow and mocking expression in the dawn's first glimmerings when she turned her animal to face him, then said, "Ready to ride, Marshal? Hope you slept well. Don't know 'bout you, but it seemed as though the people in the room next to mine had a tough time getting themselves bedded down last night. Noise level was such, I thought I never would get to close my eyes."

Longarm grunted something unintelligible, then stomped over to the line-backed dun Amos had provided for the trip. He took his own sweet time getting all his essentials loaded.

A sun the shape of a clipped fingernail and the color of molten iron made a blazing appearance on the eastern horizon, before he'd finally got himself mounted. Then the heavily armed quartet eased their animals down the main thoroughfare and out of the sleeping town.

Petey Baxter took the lead and headed the party east along the cottonwood and live oak north bank of the Palo Duro River. Longarm trailed behind Rebecca McCabe and brought up the rear. In spite of feeling as though he'd been jerked through a knothole backward, the groggy, sex-whipped lawman had trouble keeping his wandering gaze off Rebecca McCabe's tight, muscular behind as it shifted from side to side as though an integral part of the animal she rode.

Ten miles or so out of Mesquite, Baxter turned the posse south across a rock-strewn, shallow spot in the sluggish, ankle-deep river. The bleak, featureless, near-flat, eastern border of the Llano Estacado stretched out for miles ahead of them. The earth fell ever so slightly as it progressed toward the rocky bluffs of the Caprock Escarpment—a naturally formed transition area between the high, smooth plains on the west and the lower, rolling flatlands of East Texas.

Strung out in single file, sometimes several horse lengths apart, the trip offered little opportunity for idle chitchat. The terrain, resembling the top of a table at a distance, turned rugged the farther south and east the group progressed. Clumps of short, tough greenery and prairie grass receded and eventually disappeared altogether. Trees all but vanished from the desolate, stony landscape. Eons of blistering, unrelenting sun appeared to have leached the entire countryside of any color other than shades of gray, brown, tan, or a combination of those hues.

About two hours into the ride, Rebecca McCabe called

back to Longarm, "Appears God's never bothered to visit this place at all, Marshal Long. Seems a right proper spot for Simon Grimm to die, if you want my opinion."

Longarm could only nod and dab at the pools of sweat pouring from his body as a result of the previous evening's incredibly satisfying debauchery.

The posse's progress, easygoing and unhurried at the beginning, grew even slower and more problematic for the horses. In some spots, the rocky, uneven footing turned treacherous and required that they dismount and lead their animals. Near as Longarm could determine, his company of intrepid manhunters were traveling at a snail's pace of something around three miles an hour.

Well before noon, the sun hovered in a steel-colored sky like a well-polished, double-eagle gold piece heated in a crucible to the point of melting. The ambient temperature shot up to what a condemned soul might expect to find while awaiting entrance on hell's front doorstep.

At one point, Longarm reined his animal to a stop and removed his brown tweed suit coat. He secured the garment to the back of the saddle with his bedroll. Then he soaked a bandanna and tied it around his gritty, sweat-drenched neck. Feeling as though he were being broiled alive, he stared ahead in amazement at Rebecca McCabe. The bold-as-brass female looked as fresh as a daisy and totally unaffected by the sweltering heat.

But by about an hour before noon, all four riders were experiencing the undeniable sensation that the Llano Estacado had turned into something like an anvil heated to near melting by a blacksmith's blast furnace. Even the McCabe woman was soaked to the skin and had begun to exhibit more than a bit of distress.

Petey Baxter kept the roasting party of searchers moving at a slow, steady pace and didn't stop. For the most part, everyone drank from the several canteens hanging from each saddle and tended his or her particular needs on the move. It astonished Longarm more than a little that he heard not a single word of complaint from Rebecca Mc-Cabe. Near as he could tell from all outward appearances, the more tiresome and difficult their adventure into the great North Texas badlands proved, the more determined the steely eyed woman seemed to become.

Only once did the slow-moving party have to rein up long enough for the lanky, headstrong Rebecca to dismount, find a convenient spot behind a nearby boulder, and tend to her toilet. In the vast emptiness and quiet, a man would have had to have been as deaf as a post not to hear as she unburdened herself of the fluid acquired from the morning's constant attention to her canteens. The distinctive sound of what went into the sand brought a grin to Longarm's face. He readjusted his hat and glanced over at Petey and Amos. Both men hung their heads and sniggered behind grubby paws. That single delay lasted no more than a minute before the McCabe woman was back in the saddle, and everyone was on the move again.

Then, of a sudden, just before the sun hit its skin-singeing, brain-boiling, midday zenith, the vast curvature of the entire viewable planet appeared to rip apart and reveal an apocalyptic split in the earth's ancient hide. To Longarm it seemed as though the world's crust had been ripped open with a dull, crosscut saw of unimaginable enormity heated red-hot and wielded by the hand of a vengeful God.

That same laughing, playful, trickster deity had used his enormous fingers to dig innumerable canyons and raise huge cone-shaped buttes from the earth's ancient, tortured, scarred hide. He'd stacked enormous stones in bizarre ways men could not have imagined until seeing them. Placed irregular, rugged mounds of earth and stone atop endless miles of mesas. Painted it all in colors so spectacular that when set against the never-ending blue of a stark, cloudless Texas sky, the scene had the power to take the surprised viewer's breath away.

Chapter 12

By the time the dust-covered quartet drew up to the canyon's rim, Longarm's sun-roasted noggin throbbed and pounded beneath his Stetson. He watched as their guide steered his animal into the stingy shade beneath one of the half dozen or so scruffy, sun-and-wind-blasted trees clinging to precarious life near the chasm's rough, crumbling edge.

Petey Baxter stepped down, then began to fuss with his beast's rigging. He loosed the sweat-soaked cinch strap and said, "Best we all take a breather, folks. Get out of this brain-fryin' sun for a couple a hours. Rest out animals. Then we'll ease on down the trail into the canyon soon as the sun's headed a bit toward settlin' in the west—couple hours or so from now maybe. Wouldn't think as much, but it's cooler down there at the bottom. Lots a trees and helluva lot better shade along the river. More moisture in the air nearer we get to the river as well. Think you'll find it considerably more comfortable than up here in this pitiless heat."

Longarm leaned on his saddle horn for several more seconds. Stared at the stunning vista laid out for as far as a man's eye could see. He heard Rebecca say, "My God, I didn't realize Palo Duro Canyon was so vast or so beautiful."

One-eyed Petey nodded toward a wide cut in the earth not far from the clump of deformed shade trees. "Like the man once said, ever'thang's bigger in Texas, Miss McCabe. Right over yonder's a twisty piece of trail what drops 'bout eight hundred feet to the canyon floor," Petey said and continued to fuss with his animal. "What you'll find, once we get ourselves on down there, is that the Palo Duro is six miles wide in places, near a thousand feet deep, and totals over a hundred and twenty miles long—one end to the other."

"A hundred and twenty miles?" Rebecca said. "You're not kidding me, are you, Mr. Baxter? You're sure?"

"Oh, absolutely, miss," Petey said. "I've walked every inch of 'er more'n once. Not as big as that 'un out in northern Arizona, but she's impressive nonetheless. Most beautiful spot on earth far as I'm concerned. Filled with rolling, craggy hills that rise off mesas what appear to go on forever. Thousands a smaller canyons and draws seem to bleed in from ever'wheres, east and west. There's steep, dangerous bluffs, gigantic hoodoos, and caves at every turn. The combinations of colors here in the afternoon sun are nothin' short of amazin'. And, hell, there's plenty a places for a skunk like that Grimm feller to hide out, that's for damned certain, too. Pardon my language, Miss. Forgot I 'uz in mixed company there for a second."

Rebecca slid off the back of her long-legged black, then strolled to the canyon's lip. Hands resting on the butts of her brace of pistols, she threw her head back and let out a snort of a laugh. She stared into the distance, then waved Petey's apology away with, "I've seen and heard a lot. Doubt there's much of anything you could say or do that would embarrass me in the least."

Petey Baxter stopped jerking around on his saddle, raised a stubble-covered chin, then turned his one function-

132

ing eye toward the incredible scene that spread south and east before them. For several seconds, he stared into the distance as though gazing into the eyes of a lover. "Do appreciate that, miss," he said. "Like I tole you before, she's big, but if that Grimm feller's anywheres out there, I'll find him fer ya. Swear 'fore Jesus, I will."

Longarm found himself agreeing with Baxter's heartfelt assessment of the stunning landscape. From where he sat his horse, the astounding abyss appeared to roll south in an endless oceanlike panorama of tiered earth stacked like a breakfast order of pancakes comprised of numerous brilliantly colored layers of red, yellow, gray, brown, gold, and purple stone and soil. Complementing the countryside's vibrant majesty were numerous easily viewable buttes and mesas. He pointed west toward a trio of colossal spires and said, "Those peaks got names, Petey? The taller ones, I mean."

Baxter glanced in the direction of Longarm's raised finger, then nodded and said, "That biggest 'un yonder's called the Lighthouse. Not sure as whether them others has got what you could call *official* names yet. Some calls that 'un nearest the Lighthouse the Castle. And I've heard the one nearest us referred to as the Capitol, but I cain't say fer sure any of that's absolute."

As he lumbered off his tired animal's back, Amos Black said, "You got us a spot picked out to camp for the night, Petey?"

"Thought we'd try to make it down to ole Charlie Goodnight's original dugout site. Man picked a damn near perfect spot to set up when he first arrived here back in '76—bein' as how it's right next to the river and all. You know the place I'm talkin' 'bout, Amos."

"Aw, kinda. Only been there once before, myself," Black said. "Like I told Marshal Long, figure as how you know a

133

helluva lot more 'bout this place than just about anyone in the whole panhandle region. Explored this area more'n anybody I've ever met."

Petey Baxter finished with his horse, led it to the nearest scraggly juniper, then tied the beast to a low-hanging limb. He strolled up to the canyon rim, gazed down the eight-hundred foot drop, then kicked a storm cloud of rocks and clods over the edge. He swung an all-encompassing arm at the extraordinary scene before those who had followed him, pointed, and said, "Like I mentioned before, we can put our camp right down yonder by the river."

"Why that particular spot?" Longarm said.

"All this area up here—on this end of the canyon I mean—is by far the best place to lay up. Everything gets one helluva lot rougher the farther south you go. Bet you if that Grimm feller is still anywheres around these parts, he's somewheres right down there around Goodnight's campsite. Know that's where I'd be."

As Rebecca led her sleek-coated black to the shade, she said, "Then what?"

Baxter shrugged. "Well, once we've settled in, we can work our way out in ever-widening circles, scoutin' for sign. We'll find 'im."

Amos Black flopped onto the ground under a twisted, wind-seared juniper and fanned himself with his hat. "Really think you can find him, Petey?"

"Oh hell, yeah, Amos. If the no-account skunk's still around these parts, bet we pick up on the murderous Simon Grimm's trail pretty quick. Realize as how the canyon looks a mite imposin' to you folks from up here. Truth is, she's considerably tighter and a lot smaller once you get down to the bottom, and there ain't a whole buncha people down there messin' around at any one time. Leastways, not yet. All that'll probably change once Goodnight gets all his ranchin' operations going full bore." He nodded, then as if to himself he added, "Yeah, right at the end of this here trail is the best place to start lookin' for a murderin' skunk like Simon Grimm. Good water. Good grass. Great place to shelter."

Once all the animals had been moved out of the sun and picketed to a tree, Longarm, Rebecca, and Petey Baxter also selected comfortable spots in the shade, stretched out on the ground, and tried for a much-needed afternoon siesta.

Rebecca McCabe, Longarm noted, moved as far away from the men as she could get and still be protected from the sun's power. She dropped to the ground in the grudging cover provided by the most distant plant along that part of the canyon's rugged rim, pulled her fancy, crimped, Texas-style sombrero down over her eyes, and, as near as he could tell, immediately drifted off to sleep.

Much too quickly, at least it seemed so for Longarm's taste, an overly enthusiastic Petey Baxter roused everyone and had them mounted and back on their journey. The wide, almost roadlike trail they followed snaked ever downward in a series of sweeping, back-and-forth curves, loops, and cutbacks. The passage of hundreds of cattle had ground the hardened earth underfoot into a thick layer of powder-fine, reddish brown dust. And, to Longarm's surprise, even late in the day, cloudlike banks of dense fog drifted above the trees along the river and, in spots, hovered around the base of the peaks that rose from the canyon floor. On several occasions, they rode in and out of patches of the strange, curling, drifting mist.

After a nearly torturous descent, the steep path leveled out and narrowed between the canyon's westernmost wall and the welcoming trees. Then it struck out almost due south, where it veered nearer to the bank of the shallow Prairie Dog Town Fork of the Red River. The stark, multicolored, dirt palisades of the gorge created by time and wind and water erosion now loomed ominously above them. Lush groves of cottonwood, willow, juniper, and salt cedar swayed in silent, inviting abundance next to the rocky bed of the slow-moving stream that had created it all. Beneath the trees, uncountable patches of multicolored wildflowers grew in splotchy profusion in every direction.

Two hours into the descent, the pathway had contracted to the point where Longarm began to feel more than just a little bit uncomfortable. Petey Baxter didn't help the situation any when he drew everyone to a halt, sat his horse, and didn't move for almost two minutes.

Rebecca McCabe, obviously tiring of the unexplained delay, glanced around at Longarm, then cocked her head to one side and shrugged. The inquisitive lawman urged his mount around her, past a confused-looking Amos Black, and reined up next to Baxter.

"What's up, Petey?" he said, then noticed that their intrepid guide had unlimbered his Henry rifle. The cocked weapon sat propped against his leg.

At first, Baxter seemed not to have heard Longarm's question. His head swiveled from side to side in quick, jerky motions. Then, in a kind of breathy, mumbling hiss, he said, "Not sure. But somethin' just don't seem right." He nodded, then leaned forward. "See yonder on the other side of the river bed? Down 'tween all them rocks and stuff. That 'ere's Goodnight's dugout. Might not be able to detect much 'cept the top of it from here, but it's there, sure enough."

"So? What's the problem?"

"Cain't tell for certain, but listen." He tilted his head sideways like an inquisitive hound. "You hear anything odd?"

Longarm turned his ear toward Goodnight's abandoned campsite and strained to hear something wayward. "No," he said. "Nothing. Don't hear a sound."

"Yeah," Petey said, "you hit the nail right on the head. And that's the problem. There ain't no sounds at all. No birds. There's always birds down here. All kinds of other critters as well. Usually see plenty of deer, rabbits, squirrels, and such. Not far from here's where I run across them Goodnight cowboys 'fore I hightailed it to Mesquite. Today, there ain't nothin' movin'. Seems like the whole world's gone still as the bottom of a fresh-dug grave."

"You sure?"

"Hell, yes. 'S almost like there ain't nothing alive in the whole canyon. There's a breeze, can feel it on my face. But look, the leaves on the trees and bushes ain't movin'. It's as still as a sack of flour in my mama's pantry down here. River ain't but a few inches deep, and she's movin'. But I swear 'fore Jesus cain't even hear so much as a single ripple. 'S creepy weird, Marshal. Spine-chilling strange, if you ask me."

Petey Baxter gritted his teeth and hung back as Longarm urged the dun across the lazy, knee-deep stream and reined to a stop on the far bank. Goodnight's crude dugout and the cleared area around and fronting it finally came into easy view. Wedged at the sheltering base of a rock-littered hillock, the sturdy log, dirt, and slate structure's west-facing door stood open to the vagaries of weather and any inquisitive animal. For reasons Longarm couldn't readily explain, the pitch-black interior looked somewhat foreboding, in spite of the fact that the entire edifice sat in a shimmering pool of bright, reddish yellow afternoon sunlight.

As Longarm stepped from his mount, he slipped the double-action Frontier model Colt from its well-oiled holster. He heard but ignored the sound of horses splashing across the wide, shallow stream at his back. A quick perusal of the entire area seemed to reveal nothing amiss.

He dropped his mount's reins to the ground and strode toward the crude shelter's yawning front entrance. Eight or ten steps away from Goodnight's makeshift dwelling, he noticed a well-used fire pit and metal spit off to one side. He drew to a quick stop, sniffed the air, then took several steps backward. The undeniable odors of death, putrefaction, and advanced rot hung in the air. Not strong. Not overpowering. In fact, barely detectable. Just enough to make a man's mouth water. Bring a coppery taste to the tongue. Make a body's nose hairs twitch.

Afoot, Petey, Amos, and Rebecca crept up and spread out on either side of the stone-still lawman. Rebecca, standing closest to Longarm, sniffed, rubbed her nose, then said, "Didn't smell anything till I got right up here beside you, Marshal Long. What do you make of it?"

"Not sure, Miss McCabe. Could be a dead animal. Just no way of knowing till we take a closer look." He motioned with his pistol barrel and said, "Petey, you circle around behind the dugout on the left. Amos, you go right. Either of you see anything living, flush it my way. Find anything as looks suspicious, call out. Miss McCabe and I'll be there quicker'n double-greased lightning."

Petey Baxter and Amos Black disappeared into the scrub brush and knee-high patches of big bluestem grass growing on either side of and atop the improvised shelter. A pair of metallic clicks almost as loud as a drunken brush popper cracking walnuts with his fists drew Longarm's darting attention to the Greener in Rebecca McCabe's hands. The nervy girl had cocked both barrels. Wary and waiting, she stood erect with the weapon's stock snugged against her shoulder and pointed directly at the seemingly empty lodging's entrance.

Time seemed to move like a farmer with an anvil in his

bib overalls even though less than two minutes had managed to get away when Amos Black called out, "Back here, Marshal Long. Better come on around back of the dugout. Take a look at what we just found. You gotta see this."

Longarm took one step, then stopped dead in his tracks when Rebecca started to follow. "Maybe it'd be best if you let me check on what's up first, Miss McCabe."

Rebecca's sapphire-colored eyes smoldered as if a sizzling bolt of pitchfork lightning had just struck somewhere behind them. "I've seen the worst Simon Grimm can do, Custis. There's nothing behind this hole in the ground that can even compare to what that man visited on my sister and her children."

"You've said as much before."

"Well, here's something I haven't said. We had to pick up my slaughtered family's scattered remains with shovels, hoes, and two dozen burlap bags."

Longarm wagged his head back and forth like a tired dog and stared at his feet.

"Besides, if there's even the slightest chance I might get to use this big popper on Simon Grimm, I'm not about to pass on it. So don't you go worryin' yourself about me. Lead on. I'll follow, but if Grimm's back there, you'd best get the hell out of my way."

Longarm shrugged, turned, then stomped into the bushes and grass alongside the dugout. He'd rounded the corner at the rear of the temporary refuge when he almost bumped into Petey Baxter. The man's heavily scarred face was covered with a blue bandanna held close with tightly clenched fingers. Like another car in the train, Rebecca bounced off Longarm but quickly recovered, stepped to one side, then brought the shotgun's stock back up to her shoulder.

A few steps farther on, Amos Black motioned toward a

spot at the bottom of a patch of yellowed, dying grass at his feet. "Think we mighta found that missin' cowboy Petey was tellin' us about, Marshal Long."

Through his bandanna mask, Baxter mumbled, "Well, part of 'im, anyways. Not much, but a big enough part to figure as how it's probably the same one."

"What the hell are you two talking about?" Longarm said. "Whataya mean part of him?"

Black waved the inquisitive lawman forward, then stepped away from his vantage point. "Gotta get all the way over here to see what I mean, Marshal. Gets a bit ripe the closer you are, but it's quite a sight. Ain't seen nothin' like this since back in my days fightin' in Mr. Lincoln's War of Northern Aggression. Reminds me of that other lifetime I spent during a week at Gettysburg."

Longarm brought a hand up, gave Rebecca McCabe the kind of look that stopped her from advancing any farther. Then he strode to Amos Black's side. Atop a blooming bed of bent-down big bluestem grass, he saw what appeared to be a man's naked, severed leg. A badly worn boot with a fancy Mexican spur still attached graced the useless foot. No doubt about it in Longarm's racing mind. The entire amputation could not have been accomplished with anything other than a well-honed, double-bit ax.

Chapter 13

Amos Black scanned everything around them except the amputated limb. His gaze darted to the tops of hills, then to trees, bushes, boulders, nearby ridges. "Looks like it was chopped off at the hip to me, Long. Bit of rot up there where it was removed." He stopped searching their surroundings and leaned close to Longarm's ear. "'S what we smelled," he hissed. "Can you imagine such a thing? Can only guess, but looks to me like some crazy sonofabitch mighta kept this poor bastard alive for nigh on a week. Then chopped him up like firewood kindlin'."

"Damnation," Longarm said. The shocked deputy marshal took half a step backward and whipped out his own bandanna. He held the block of red material over twitching nostrils and said, "Think it's been layin' here very long, Amos?"

Black shook his leonine head and fingered the hammers on his shotgun. "No. Not really. Would seem as how it'd be a lot farther along toward really festerin' if'n it'd been here more'n a day or two. What really surprises the bejabbers outta me is that no animals have got their hooks on a chunk of meat that big as yet. 'S almost like . . ." Black appeared

141

to drift off into thought, then turned and began eyeballing the very same areas of the canyon that he had already scanned. "'S almost like . . ." he muttered, then trailed off again.

"Like what, for crying out loud," Longarm hissed from under his bandanna. "Quit dancin' around. What the hell are you thinkin'?"

Black didn't move, but continued his concentrated search. "'S almost like someone put it here so we would find it. Then waited. Kept all the wild animals away just to make certain. 'S almost like . . . someone wanted to watch when we came on it."

Longarm tensed, eased back several steps, then ran a darting glance over the same spots Amos had previously gone over. "Ain't nothing out there. I don't see a single thing amiss, Amos."

"What's wrong with you two?" Rebecca called out, then started toward them.

Petey Baxter grabbed the surprised girl by the arm and tried to pull her away from the scene. Rebecca snatched her shirtsleeve from Petey's grasp and strode to Longarm's side. A quick glance at the amputated limb was all she needed.

Rather matter-of-factly, she tilted her head to one side, as though thinking, then said, "Hate to say it, boys, but I've seen this exact kind of thing before. In point of actual fact, I've seen a hell of a lot worse. Nothing new here for me. Truth is, I expected something just like this if we got anywhere close to Grimm. He's left bodies, parts of bodies, just like this, all the way from Utah Territory to this very spot."

Baxter dropped his bandanna long enough to gasp, "Why would anyone leave a man's severed leg just a-layin' around on the ground? Looks to me almost like it was deliberately placed there, don't you think? I mean, look at it. 'S like a

142

chunk a meat put on display in a butcher shop. If Grimm did this, he was proud of hackin' this poor sonofabitch to pieces and wanted us to know it."

"Well, if'n you wanted to fool yourself, maybe you could reason as how an animal come on this poor feller when he 'uz already dead. Critter ripped the leg off, dragged it here, and left it for later," Amos said. "I've seen as much before. Bear, big cat, wolf, hell any of 'em coulda left the leg layin' around jus' like this."

"You see any bear, big cat, or wolf sign 'round that piece a man meat, Amos?" Petey snapped.

Black studied the scene for several more seconds, then muttered, "Truth is, I can't see any sign at all, Petey. Almost like the thing got dropped from somewhere up in heaven or maybe just appeared here like some kinda wicked magic. I mean, a set of goofy circumstances like droppin' from heaven makes as much sense as an animal draggin' it up and leavin' it. But, the truth is, I ain't ever seen any animal livin' as coulda removed a leg the way this 'un came off. Naw, poor sonofabitch what lost this leg had it chopped off."

Longarm waved in the direction of the odiferous glob of festering rot with his pistol, then said, "We can't be worryin' 'bout such incidentals right now, folks. Don't really matter how the man's leg got here. Let's get it in the ground. Cover this spot with some fresh dirt to knock the odor down. Get our camp set up. Pitch-dark's gonna be on us 'fore we know it. Think we'd best get prepared for whatever might have waited for us to show up."

The nervous party sprang into a fit of concentrated action for as long as the dying sunlight held out. Amos disposed of the poor cowboy's severed limb and covered the spot where they'd discovered it with a pile of freshly dug earth. Longarm, Petey, and Rebecca scrounged up as much in the way of fallen timber as they could find beneath the tree-lined riverbank, dragged it all up around the dugout's entrance, and built a low wall.

In fairly short order, by working at a feverish pace, the posse had constructed a scrappy but serviceable four-foot-high defensive enclosure. The stack of limbs and other tree trash lay in a rough semicircle that started on either side of the dugout's front entrance and bulged toward the river for about twenty feet like a giant, wooden horseshoe.

When it appeared they'd done all they could until the following morning, Longarm called everyone to a spot near the dugout's fire pit. He rubbed a sweat-dripping nose on his shirtsleeve, resettled his Stetson, then said, "We'll picket our animals up here, as close to us as we can get 'em, just outside our new wall. That way we can keep our eyes and ears on 'em, and it'll be the easiest spot to get at if anything tries to bother 'em."

"We could sleep in the dugout, couldn't we?" Petey said. "Seems to me we'd be even safer in there. Got our new wall 'round the door and all that dirt and rock 'tween us and any kinda hurt. Might be safer still. Whatcha think?"

Rebecca McCabe had already pitched her saddle and bedroll onto the ground next to the fire pit. She pointed and said, "You boys can do whatever you want about puttin' it down for the night. Right there's where I'm sleeping, next to a stoked-up fire, just out of the light. I'm not about to make my bed in that scorpion-infested pit of a dugout. Saw one of those ugly critters in there while the sun was still out—nearly as big as my hand. Stinger-tailed bug that big could put a hurtin' on a draft horse. Take my chances out here on the ground."

"Don't know 'bout you boys, but I'm sleepin' out here beside the fire, too," Longarm said as he glanced at his bedroll and realized that Rebecca had placed her gear as near to his as she could and still have a few feet between them. "Rebecca's right. Inside of that dugout ain't fit for human habitation right now. Take us a week of hard work to get it back into any kind of livable condition. If it shakes out that we might have to stay any longer than a few days, might want to consider doing exactly that. But right now, I think we're all better off out here where we can hear anything that might go amiss."

Amos Black toed at the dirt and nodded. "Sounds like a good enough plan to me. But once we've had a bite to eat and rested up a bit, might be a good idea to post a lookout all night long, Marshal. Hour on, three hours off, for each of us. Military fashion, you know. Should work out just fine for everybody."

"Sounds good to me. Sure as hell wouldn't want the crazy bastard what left that leg back yonder a-sneakin' up on us while we sleep," Petey added. "This here little fort we've built's okay for somethin' temporary like, you know. Makes me feel some safer, but I'd feel a whole bunch better long as someone's up watchin' over us."

"Won't be any moon tonight," Amos Black said. "Gonna be so dark away from our fire you won't be able to find your own nose with both hands."

Longarm took the first hour's watch. Woke Rebecca for the second. As he was the only one with a serviceable timepiece of any kind, he agreed that they should pass it from person to person during that seemingly endless first night.

No one slept well. All talk died out as soon as black dark settled in. Amos Black tossed and turned in his bedding as though troubled by bad dreams. On several occasions, Longarm heard Petey Baxter groan like a man being tortured with a hot poker. Rebecca McCabe didn't appear to have closed her eyes at all and was so anxious to stand her watch that she relieved Longarm before his initial hour had even expired.

"I've still got about fifteen minutes to go. You didn't have to get up so quick," he said and handed her his big-ticking Ingersoll pocket watch.

"Understand completely, Custis," she said and slipped the turnip-sized timepiece into the pocket of fringed leather jacket she had put on against the desert's nighttime cold. They stood just outside the illumination cast by their camp's glowing fire, when she added, "Just can't get comfortable. Not sure why, but have to admit that there's something in the air that stirs a sense of unease in me unlike any I've ever felt before. Guess I should have expected such feelings now that I'm so close to Grimm."

Longarm peered over the dwindling coals that flickered in the fire pit, then stared into the impenetrable blackness of the all-encompassing moonless night. He could hear the movements of their picketed animals as they stamped iron-shod feet and nervously moved about. He swung a piercing gaze into the McCabe woman's cobalt eyes. "Tell you the truth, Rebecca, I think you're right. Figure what we're feeling is nothing more than the presence of Simon Grimm. Wouldn't surprise me in the least to discover he's watching our every move right this very moment."

Rebecca reacted almost as though she'd been slapped. She sucked in a gasping breath, took half a step backward, then brought her double-primed Greener up against a slender hip and cocked both barrels. "This is the closest I've managed to get to him so far, Custis. Didn't have any inkling mere proximity to the murderous skunk would have such a profound effect on me."

"We'd probably all feel better if it weren't so dark. With a cloudless sky and a good moon, we should easily be able to see that spectacular pillar of rock Petey pointed out earlier today. As it is, a body gets out a few feet past our scrappy wall, and it's blacker'n the inside of a solid bronze coffin."

Right at the end of his second tour of guard duty that night, just as he handed the Ingersoll to Rebecca again, from somewhere in the inky shadows that engulfed them, a spine-tingling, chattering howl swept over their protective barrier like an enormous crashing wave. The unholy wail was followed by strange, moaning laughter that sounded as though it rose from the sulfurous bowels of Satan's fiery pit. The insane sniggering sent their already nervous animals into a fit of frenetic movement. They snorted, tossed their heads, strained against taut picket ropes, and pawed at the dusty ground. Even Rebecca's audacious black whinnied, stomped its shiny feet, and kicked at the rocky soil.

"Jesus," Rebecca murmured under her breath as she instinctively brought the Greener up to a firing position and moved closer to Longarm.

The audacious deputy marshal placed a quieting hand atop the weapon's barrels, then hissed, "*Sssh*. Quiet, 'Becca. Be still. Try not to move for a few seconds."

The howling and laughter slowly died out as though carried away on an unfelt breeze. "How far do you think he is from us? Sounds really close," Rebecca whispered.

"Impossible to tell." Longarm barely breathed. "Could be a quarter of a mile. Could be right outside the wall. Dark like this can sometimes fool you when it comes to sound and distance. Need to have him cackle again. Maybe we'd get a better fix on a possible direction."

Within seconds, another spate of hideous wailing trailed by a muffled series of ebbing whoops and something that sounded like, "*Snick, snick, snickety, snick*," spread over them from within the night's all-enveloping gloom. Rebecca followed Longarm as he strode to the inner curve of their wall. They stood for several seconds, listening ears turned toward the strange sounds that seemed to float down on them from somewhere overhead.

Then, of a sudden, a keening screech that sent cold, sweat-drenched, chill bumps up and down Longarm's spine dropped on the couple as though definitely cast from a spot above and slightly to the west. Rebecca McCabe moved so close he could feel her arm against his.

"Sounds like a woman screaming," she hissed. "For the love of God, Long, that's a woman."

Amos Black sprang from his bedding. He grabbed his big boomer, then, bootless, stumbled to Longarm's side. "Sweet Virginia, ain't heard nothin' like that since havin' to suffer through a long, miserable night after a particularly brutal day of battle during the Big War. Sounds just like them poor boys we had to leave out on the field 'cause we couldn't find 'em in the daylight."

The thin, high-pitched shrieking started anew. It rose to an ear-piercing level, then abruptly stopped again. "God Almighty," Rebecca said. "Sounded like the poor woman's mouth had something clamped over it."

Longarm pointed into the dark. "Honest to God, folks, seems to be coming from the direction of that pile of rocks and dirt Petey called the Lighthouse. Soon as black dark turns to light, I think we should fog outta here. Head that direction quick as our feet can carry us. Get up there. Find out what the hell's goin' on. If Grimm's captured a woman, we can save her before he's had a chance to take her life. Maybe."

Amos said, "Talbot Butterworth didn't mention one word 'bout no missin' woman from Mesquite, as I recollect."

"No," Longarm agreed.

Amos swung the barrel of his shotgun at the wall of blue black dark outside their protective barrier. "But there ain't no place else she could've come from, Long. No other town within fifty miles of here. Must be somebody missin' from Mesquite that Butterworth don't know about."

"Anything's possible," Longarm said, then pulled his pocket watch. "'S after three. Should be seein' daylight in two, two and a half hours, or so. Want to get up and get on the move quick as we can, once we can see again." As he stomped back toward the fire pit and whatever might remain in their coffeepot, he added, "Any way possible to save that poor screamin' wretch, we've got to get after it."

Longarm poured a cup of steaming belly wash that had achieved a consistency similar to molasses. He took a sip, then glanced toward the dugout. Pistol in one hand, rifle on his crossed legs, Petey Baxter sat in the crude shelter's doorway. The one-eyed man's twisted, scarred face appeared frozen in a mask of wild, unsettled fear.

"Ain't movin' from this here spot till I can see somethin', Long. Hard enough trick with two eyes. Dark as it is, it's damned near impossible with only one," Petey said, then pulled his enormous bowie knife and stabbed it into the ground beside him.

As night staggered toward morning, the unseen woman's tortured screaming slackened. Then, for a while, another round of hair-curling shrieks assaulted Longarm and his party in sporadic bursts that pierced the quiet dark like a sharpened ice pick. Longarm retired to his bedding during the unsettling ordeal and fought to stay awake. Rebecca McCabe did the same and occasionally covered both ears with her hands. Petey Baxter fidgeted with his weapons in his dugout doorway nest, but never moved outside its security. Amos Black raged around behind the wall, shook his fists, cursed the impenetrable gloom, Simon Grimm, the screaming woman, and anything else he could lay his talented tongue on. Then, about an hour before the sun peeked over the eastern horizon, the agonized screeches ceased their ghastly assault altogether, as though a stark and gruesome curtain had finally fallen.

Chapter 14

With the first rays of good light, Longarm and Rebecca followed as Baxter and Black scouted a trail in the direction of the previous evening's terror. They watched as the two old canyon rats studied every overturned rock, every scruff mark on the uneven stony ground, every bent blade of grass, and every broken tree twig for indications of human presence or passing.

After much cussing and discussing, Petey pointed toward the Lighthouse and said, "He's up there, alright. Bet my horse on it. They's several good-sized caves up on the mesa where that pile a rocks is sittin'. We get ourselves on up there, maybe we can kill the crazy sonofabitch and save that poor screamin' woman—if she's still alive."

Amos Black glanced at Longarm, scratched his beard, then nodded and growled, "Sounds like as good a plan as any to me, Marshal Long. Don't want that poor soul to go through another torture session like the one she had to endure last night, and we had to listen to. Skin's still crawlin' 'round on my body like it ain't even attached from havin' to hear all that screamin' and sufferin'. Truth is, I ain't heard nothin' to match it since back in the days when I 'uz a kid an we 'uz fightin' the Comanche."

By the time a blazing sun painted the color of fresh blood could rise high enough in the sky to fully illuminate the canyon's stark, beautiful floor, Longarm's band of searchers had managed to scramble to a spot near the flattened base of the Castle—the peak nearest the Lighthouse. Forced to give up on their horses because of the rough, sharp, uneven footing, the entire party had expended considerable energy as they slogged their way up from their camp on the river. Tired and ready for a break, they halted atop the rust-colored platform the craggy dirt-and-rock Castle stood upon.

After nearly an hour of welcomed inactivity in any splotch of handy shade, Longarm and Rebecca continued to relax and wait while the other two men forged ahead. They had all agreed on a plan for Amos and Petey to swing around on the west side of the looming Lighthouse. Longarm and Rebecca would continue in from the north, then veer to the east, thereby encircling the entire pedestal-like formation from which Palo Duro's most impressive natural spire rose.

Sweating and covered in a crust of reddish yellow dust, Longarm took a swig from his canteen, then passed it to Rebecca. He wiped dripping lips on his shirtsleeve, then said, "Could actually work the way we've got it planned. Get Grimm circled in. We might well end this nightmare right here, today. Kill or capture the crazy sonofabitch like Petey said. Just hope maybe we're in time to help that poor woman—but I wouldn't bet on it."

Rebecca took a sip of the water, then handed the canteen back to her partner. "Well, I'm gonna pray you're right, Marshal Long," she said, then snatched up the shotgun she had propped against a handy boulder. "Nothing more I'd rather see today than Simon Grimm's bullet-riddled body stretched out in a blood-soaked patch of this near-lifeless earth beneath my feet."

With Longarm in the lead, and the punishing sun nigh on directly overhead, they struck out again. Picked their way down a steep, treacherous slope littered with shifting, broken piles of sharp, jagged stone. Then they carefully edged upward again along a barely discernible trail that ran past scrubby patches of sumac, star thistle, and mesquite. From there, the path led them along a narrow ridge that abruptly plunged into a series of deep million-year-old ravines carved by rushing water. Water that had vanished eons before.

After almost two hours to torturous up-and-down climbing along an easy-to-follow trail that Amos and Petey had already marked out for them, Longarm and Rebecca finally reached a broad, open mesa. Covered in another layer of grit and sweat, and appearing somewhat worse for wear, Rebecca flopped onto a convenient rock, snatched her hat off, and fanned a glistening face.

Longarm turned to offer water again and immediately noticed a definite change in the flush-faced female's expression. Of a sudden, the bold woman who had strode into Mesquite's Top Hat Saloon like she owned it appeared touched by disbelief and frozen in place. While he watched, a look of stark surprise and creeping terror slowly etched its way across Rebecca's confused countenance. She raised a trembling arm and pointed.

Longram's hand went to the ivory grips of his Frontier model Colt. He swiveled at the waist to follow the line of the woman's shocked gaze and quaking finger. At first, he could not discern exactly what had sent his companion into such a state of obvious dismay. Only after several seconds of studying a deeply shaded area located at the bottom of the weather-hewn Lighthouse's flesh-colored rocky foundation was he able to separate human horror from its natural surroundings.

Seated amidst a camouflaging array of red and yellow Indian blanket and wildflowers that decorated a two-and-a-half-foot-tall patch of switchgrass, Longarm detected the shocking, outlined figure of a female. Stark naked, she appeared covered from toe to crown in what looked like a crusted layer of peeling, dried, scabbed-over blood. On first glance, the stunned lawman would have sworn before Jesus, on a stack of Bibles, that the woman was stone dead. But, of a sudden, the ghastly statue's blank, unseeing eyes closed, then slowly reopened.

Longarm and Rebecca reached the grisly woman's side at the same instant. The dipped-in-blood female offered no resistance when they took her by the elbows and gently lifted her from the grassy nest. Obviously in a state of the most extreme distress, they ushered the mute woman to a more accessible and comfortable spot. Helped her sit near the base of an enormous boulder that provided the entire trio with shelter from the unrelenting sun's blistering assault.

An offer of water to the wooden-featured female was met with stunned, stone-faced indifference. Closer inspection revealed the reasons for the unfortunate's glassy-eyed, lethargic demeanor. Longarm shook his head and made sounds like a growling animal as he examined the woman's badly abused body.

"Good Christ, look," Rebecca said as she picked gobs of scabs from the wretched female's hair. "Her ears are missing, for the love of God. Grimm's gone and cut both of 'em off. Sweet merciful Father, looks like he must've taken them with a dull saw blade."

Longarm held one of the pitiful female's hands up and muttered, "Along with both little fingers and her little toes."

Rebecca covered her mouth with the back of one hand. She cast a quick glance at the wretched, bloody, damaged feet and groaned. She snatched Longarm's canteen off his shoulder, quickly opened it, and doused her kerchief with the life-giving liquid. Then, with great tenderness, she wiped the dazed woman's gore-encrusted brow.

"How in the name of all that's holy can anyone in his right mind commit such wicked acts?" she muttered and tried to wipe away the caked, blackish brown, scablike buildup from near invisible eyebrows.

As if suddenly preoccupied by something unseen, Longarm rose to his feet, then reached toward Rebecca. "Hand me the shotgun. Now. Give it to me now." He grabbed the weapon away from his stunned partner, thumbed both knurled hammers back, and scanned the entire area around their shaded refuge. "'S just too easy," he hissed. "Too much like finding that butchered cowboy's leg behind the dugout. Almost like we've been deliberately lured into stopping here to help this ill-fated wretch."

Rebecca halted her attempts to cleanse their new ward's face, gently wrapped the damp kerchief around the most damaged of the unresponsive woman's hand, then stood and pulled both her heavy pistols. She cocked the weapons and hissed, "Well, if Simon Grimm's that damned smart, let 'im come on in right now."

For the next five minutes neither of the broken woman's tense protectors moved anything but their eyes. Longarm's breathing shallowed to the point where almost no sound came from his barely moving chest. Rebecca's pointed gaze darted from bush and boulder to ravine mouth and cliff face, then back again. Nothing. Nothing moved. Even the ever-present restless canyon breezes had ominously faded away. The uncomfortable silence that pressed down on them came nigh on to being overwhelming.

"Shit," Rebecca finally snorted, then holstered her pistol with a fancy gunman's spin. "He ain't comin', Long. Bet the sorry skunk's hid out somewhere watching us. Laughing into his fists like some kind of deranged, murderous beast."

Still staring hard for anything that might move, Longarm said, "Sure. Could be watchin', no doubt about it. But he ain't laughin'. Leastways, I can't hear 'im."

"We've got far more important fish to fry right at the moment," Rebecca snapped. "Gotta get this poor brutalized lady back down to Goodnight's dugout. See to her physical welfare." Hands on hips in an aggressive, angry stance, Rebecca frowned and shook her head. "Not sure we can help much with the state of her mind. But, maybe, we still have enough time to save her from a horrible death. Gonna take something like a heaven-sent miracle, if you ask me. Still and all, we have to try. A whole turn of the world for her might all depend on whether we can get these wounds cleaned up and bandaged in time."

Longarm cast a quick glance at the terribly injured woman. "Gettin' this gal back down to the river's edge is gonna be a pretty slick trick, Rebecca. Look at 'er. She's in no fit state to walk, not with wounds like those on her feet. Couldn't hobble ten steps 'thout fallin' flat on her face in all this hardscrabble shit we just trudged through. And that's even if she had the strength left to try."

"I know, Long. I know. You're preaching to the choir here. Process won't be easy, and full weight of it'll be on your shoulders."

Longarm let the hammers down on Rebecca's big popper, then handed the weapon back to her. "Figure I'm probably gonna have to carry her most, if not all, the way. Could very well take us till full dark to get back down to camp from way up here."

Rebecca patted the lawman on the shoulder. "If I could carry her myself I would, Long. Swear I would. But no doubt about it, it looks like you're the man."

"Yeah, well, it was hard enough for us to make our own way up here with no real load other than a little water and our firearms to carry. Way I've got it figured, gettin' her down and watchin' out for our own safety as well's gonna be tougher'n blowin' smoke rings down the neck of an empty whiskey bottle."

Brow furrowed, with pained wrinkles forming at the corners of each eye, Rebecca uncharacteristically looked as though she might burst into tears when she said, "Look, I know it won't be easy. But it has to be done. Just isn't any other way around the problem. You think you can actually carry the poor thing all the way back to camp, Long?"

Longarm studied his feet for several seconds, toed at dirt clods, then placed a soothing hand on Rebecca's shoulder and gave her a sympathetic pat. He said, "Well, I can sure enough try. You help me get 'er on her feet, I'll move 'round in front. Then we'll drape her arms over my shoulders till I can get her legs around me and latch on real good. No bigger'n this pathetically unlucky lady is, the trip shouldn't be all that problematic—'cept in the middle of that piece of loose shale and broken rock 'bout halfway down."

The trek back to Goodnight's dugout proved more challenging than Longarm had expected. While his lifeless human cargo didn't weigh all that much, the woman couldn't or wouldn't offer anything like helpful cooperation in the effort. And, because Rebecca had the responsibility of watching their backs, she could provide him with little in the way of a helping hand.

On several regrettable occasions, the wounded, bleeding

woman slipped from his grasp and dropped to the ground. To his stunned amazement, she made no attempt to keep herself from hitting the deck like a sackful of lead bird shot.

The time spent getting her reloaded burned more daylight than either Longarm or Rebecca liked. Given the knowledge of what might be trailing them, the dying sun urged both to perform feats of physical prowess neither would have dared claim before that fateful evening.

Chapter 15

When the near-exhausted lawman finally staggered into the sheltering surround of the camp's thrown-together stick-and-log wall, Rebecca helped him lower their charge into the comfort and cover of her own bedding. Then, once again, she quickly set to cleansing the injured woman's wounds.

By the time his partner had finished with her gruesome project, Longarm had bathed himself in the river. Dark shadows lengthened under a rising, slivered fingernail of a moon. Still, Amos and Petey had not yet made it back. Perhaps worse, not even a single sign of them had turned up.

Nearly two hours after arriving back in camp, Longarm squatted just out of the fire pit's light ring and sipped on a cup of fresh coffee. He had stood guard while valiant Rebecca had washed herself in the river, and with great effort he successfully fought off the urge to take a secret peek at her naked, inviting flesh. Now full dark came down around them like a slamming door. He glanced into the deepening blackness and watched Rebecca's futile efforts at enticing their injured ward to at least take a tiny bit of liquid.

Longarm pulled a nickel cheroot from his jacket pocket and stoked it to life. As he snapped the flaming lucifer between his fingers, then flipped it into the smoldering coals, sounds of violent movement in the bushes near the river caused icy chills to run up and down his spine. He came to his feet in a flash and unlimbered the Colt that lay across his belly.

Rebecca darted to his side, cocked shotgun at the ready. "Think it's Grimm?" she whispered.

"Doubt it," he said. "Whoever or whatever it is, it's makin' way too much racket. Doubt Grimm'd telegraph his presence like this, but anything's possible."

Pistol in hand, he urged Rebecca to a spot slightly behind him. Fully alert and primed for action, they listened as the sounds of something extremely large moved ever closer. Of a sudden, a huge section of their wall at the most extreme bend in the protective horseshoe appeared to explode. Limbs, logs, and tree flew into the night sky as though a stick of dynamite had exploded beneath them. Longarm and Rebecca leveled their weapons and readied themselves for a blistering gunfight. Amos Black crashed through the rough opening, stumbled to the edge of the fire pit, then dropped to his knees.

Longarm could not believe what his eyes told him had to be true. The bearish man's enormous hat had vanished. His shirt looked as though it had been run through a wheat thrasher. The tattered garment hung on Black in a confusion of frizzed threads. Where the shirt's material no longer covered Amos's body, Longarm could see a crop of deep, bloody scratches. Patches of the man's hair appeared to have been snatched out by the roots. One foot was minus its boot. To Deputy U.S. Marshal Custis Long, all outward signs indicated that the formidable Amos Black had just spent a number of hours in the throes of sheer panic.

Black grabbed an empty cup, reached for the coffeepot, and, with a hand as steady as a blacksmith's anvil, poured the hot liquid into it. But as he tried to sip the steaming liquid, the cup began to shake so badly he was forced to hold it in both his enormous paws.

Longarm squatted across the flames from Billy Vail's old friend, then said, "Where's Petey, Amos?"

Black's vacant gaze fixed on the fire's glowing coals. He seemed reluctant to look at Longarm. His expressionless stare didn't leave the fire when he said, "Don't know. Truly, don't know."

Longarm glanced up at Rebecca, then back at his giant of a deputy. "Whaddya mean, you don't know?"

"Not sure."

"Amos," Rebecca said, "you're not making any sense. Can you realize that? Do you understand how you sound?"

Black downed a long swig from the steaming cup, threw the remainder of the liquid into the fire, then struggled to his feet. The empty tin vessel dangled from one finger when he said, "Musta been runnin' for hours tryin' to get back down here to something like sanity. 'S easy to get lost in the dark when you're not all that familiar with the landscape." Absentmindedly, he scratched at a scabbed spot on one arm. "Must a run through ever' sticker bush 'tween here and the Castle. Fell down a couple a times. Rolled around like some kinda crazy, scared shitless kid."

Rebecca moved to the big man's side and placed one hand on his hairy arm. "Are you okay, Amos?"

Black wagged his head back and forth. He swayed in place like a confused grizzly. "Not sure, Miss McCabe. God's truth, just really not sure."

Longarm stood. "Did you find Simon Grimm's hideout?"

Somehow, Amos appeared to nod and shake his massive head at the same time. "Yeah. Could be. Well, I think so. Hell, can't really say for sure. Cave over on the west side of the Lighthouse. Number of 'em up there, you know."

"Sounds like Petey hit the nail right on the head then, didn't he?" Longarm said.

Amos nodded. "Yeah. Hit the nail on the head. Yeah, he did. But I ain't so certain it's gonna ever matter to him one way or the other."

Rebecca squeezed the big man's arm. "Why's that, Amos?"

A shaking hand pushed trembling fingers through the matted hair on his head as Black said, "Well, ain't so sure he's alive no more, Miss McCabe."

Across the flickering fire, Custis Long and Rebecca McCabe exchanged confused, questioning looks.

"What makes you think he might not be alive?" Longarm said.

Black squatted by the fire again and poured another cup of coffee. He shoved the pot back into its spot over the coals, then sipped at the scalding liquid. "Like I said before, Petey led me to the entrance of a cave located over on the west side of the Lighthouse . . ."

Longarm made impatient "go ahead" motions with one hand and said, "Yeah, yeah. You're doin' good. Get on with it. Tell us the rest."

Rebecca kneeled beside Black and placed an arm across his thick, muscular shoulders. "Go ahead, Amos. You're amongst friends here. You can tell us what happened."

Black flicked corner-of-the-eye, uneasy glances up at Longarm and then Rebecca. "Was right on the verge of gettin' dark, time we finally got to the spot Petey had in mind. I said we should set up near the entrance of the cave and just wait, or maybe even get the hell on back to camp. Petey 'uz all fired up to go inside, kill Grimm, get his corpse by the heels, and drag 'im down here."

"If I had been with the two of you, I'd of voted to wait outside myself," Rebecca said.

Amos nodded as though he had listened but not actually heard what the sympathetic woman said. "Christ, don't know what put the burr up his ass, but ole Petey'd been fired up ever since we split with you two up there by the Castle. Anyhow, tried my best to talk him out of goin' inside that cave. Argued for near ten minutes 'bout it." Then Black mumbled off into another long pause.

For near a minute the only thing Longarm heard was the burning wood as it crackled in the fire pit. Eventually, his bruised and battered deputy fished a stick from the flames and began absentmindedly digging in the coals. Then he said, "Never liked cramped places, you know. Have this thing 'bout tight spots, 'specially caves. Ain't nothin' else in the world like the feelin' comes over me when placed anywhere too cramped for me to move around."

In an all-too-obvious effort to calm her friend, Rebecca said, "Everybody's afraid of something, Amos."

Black gave a vague nod of the head, then said, "Can't imagine where the fear comes from. Ain't afraid a nothin' else in this world. Livin' or dead. But, damn, just hate a small room, narrow hallway, or tight passage like a cave. Guess it might have somethin' to do with dreams of dyin' and the grave and such. Just ain't sure."

"Okay," Longarm grunted. "You couldn't stop Petey. Had to follow him into a hole in the ground. That the deal?"

"Yeah. Guess you could put it that way. Anyhow, when we got up to the entrance, damn near passed out from the smell. Hadn't had an odor like that up my nose since cleanin' poor dead troopers off'n battlefields durin' the war. Dredged the whole horror of that particular thing back up from memories I'd suppressed ever since Gettysburg. Set to gaggin' soon's I stepped inside the damned place."

"Didn't see or hear anything?" Longarm said.

"Nothin'. Mighty dark at first. Then I noticed a weak

glow way down inside the earth. Didn't help my ability to see any, though. Hadn't gone far when Petey stopped. Kinda backed up and asked if I'd heard anything. Hadn't heard nothin', 'cept the noise all them bones made when we walked on 'em."

"Bones?" Rebecca said.

Amos stared into the fire's dying flames and nodded. "Bones, Miss McCabe Lots of 'em. Seemed to be scattered around on the floor of the cave like some kinda hideous skeletal carpet or somethin'. Kept stumblin' over 'em. Couldn't really see what kinda bones, but I am pretty damned sure what we lurched over was bones, not tree limbs or some other such debris."

"Well, what happened then?" Longarm said.

Black picked at a scabbed over scratch on his nose, then said, "Kept stumblin' 'round in the dark like a couple a blind drunks. Of a sudden, Petey stopped again, backed into me, and almost knocked me down. Went to cussin' him for bein' stupid. Then I heard this whistlin' racket, an odd *thwackin'* sound and somethin' hit me in the chest. Petey kinda grunted, then went to screamin' like a gutshot panther. Dropped to one knee to see if I could pick up whatever'd bounced off'n me. Same whistlin' racket went over my head 'bout the time I latched onto what felt like a human arm and hand. Whatever was swinging around ricocheted off the wall. Made a loud *ka-chingin'* sound."

"Jesus," Longarm mumbled.

"A human arm? You're sure, Amos?" Rebecca said.

"Sure as a man who couldn't see his hand in front of his face can be. Tell you the God's truth folks, Simon Grimm must have eyes like some kinda Mexican fruit bat, or somethin'. I jumped up and went to runnin'. Could still hear Petey screamin' when I got back outside. Didn't stop chuggin' till I got across the river yonder."

Longarm shook his head and said, "That's gotta be the most amazing tale I've ever heard."

Rebecca McCabe sprang to her feet. "Amazing? Nothing *amazing* about it. 'S damned awful if you ask me. Sounds like our friend Petey Baxter's layin' in a cave up there somewhere around the Lighthouse rendered out to nothing more'n a pile of fleshy kindling."

"True," Longarm said. "But there's nothing much we can do about it right now."

"Ain't that a fact," Amos Black snorted. "Damned if I'll be goin' back up there in the dark. Whole time I 'uz running, I kept thinking as how the sonofabitch was gonna catch up, hit me in the head, and be chewin' on a piece of my meatiest haunch by tomorrow mornin'."

Rebecca kicked dirt into the fire, then stomped back and forth as though about to burst. She stopped and shook a finger at Longarm and Amos. "You've gotta go back," she said. "We can't leave Petey up there with a human flesh-eatin' monster like Simon Grimm."

Longarm strode to his bedroll and flopped onto it. He pushed around on his saddle in an effort to make putting his head down a bit more comfortable. He rolled onto his back and pulled his hat over tired eyes. "Let's all get some rest. We'll go back up first thing in the morning. Can't do anything now. Could probably find the cave, but ain't much we can do in the dark."

Those words had barely passed Longarm's lips when the screaming started. High, thin, almost reedlike and distant at first. Then louder and more insistent as it echoed off the canyon walls, got magnified, and funneled down into the camp. Soon, Petey Baxter's tortured screeching, though nearly two miles away—as the proverbial crow flies—became damned near unbearable.

Longarm hopped to his feet, pulled his own shotgun and

165

a bag of shells. "Get yourself armed, Amos. No way in hell itself can I lie here all night listening to that. Thought I could just wait till mornin' to make the trek back up there, but not with the man screechin' like that. Just can't."

In the flickering light of the campfire, Amos Black looked stricken. "You're not kiddin'? Serious? You wanna go back up there in the dark?"

Longarm's big blaster made a loud metallic click when he breeched the weapon and dropped two loads of heavy-gauge buckshot into it. "Yep. But brighter out tonight than last night. Think we can find our way back to where you left Petey. Besides, as long as Petey's yellin' we know one thing for damned sure."

"What's that?" Rebecca said.

"Simon Grimm's busy doin' the Devil's work and won't have time to show up on the trail to the Lighthouse and stop us. Get up there as quick as we can, there's always the possibility we can save Petey. Hide in our bedrolls, and he'll die for damned sure."

"What about me?" Rebecca said.

"You'll have to stay here with that poor woman. Would be sinful to leave her alone in the kinda shape she's in."

Rebecca ran a hand through her hair. "No. That won't do. I think I should go along with you."

Longarm got right up in the agitated woman's face. "You've got to stay behind, Rebecca. This time around you just can't go with us. You know that, don't you?"

The defeated girl's shoulders sagged. She sighed, then flounced over to check on their earless, fingerless, toeless ward. She knelt next to the damaged woman and quickly went back to bathing her numerous wounds.

"God Above, help me," Amos Black said, then stomped to his saddlebags and pulled out a fresh shirt and second pair of boots. He ripped what was left of the old garment off, then pulled the new one over his head. As he stuffed the tail of the fresh piece of clothing into his pants, he muttered, "The Devil's a mighty busy feller, ain't he, Long?"

"That he is," Longarm said as he snatched up several recently freshened canteens. "Leastways he's one busy sonofabitch in Palo Duro Canyon on this particular night."

Chapter 16

The torturous trek back to the Lighthouse proved a bit easier and less knotty than either Longarm or Amos Black had
expected. A full moon would have helped, but luckily, a
crystal-clear, cloudless sky enhanced the available moonlight. Unfortunately, every time either man glared toward
the ominous, shadowy spire that split the night sky above
them like a sharpened scythe, they were greeted with peals
of skin-tingling human screeches.

Reflected and amplified by endless stretches of the
canyon's sandy floor, the moon's weak glow slowed their
journey somewhat, but it still allowed them to travel almost
at a pace that they could have expected in the middle of the
day. During the entire slogging haul, Petey Baxter's unsettling shrieks continued to wax and wane. His distant, high,
thin squealing came nigh on to fading completely away on
several occasions. Then, preceded by a singularly lengthy
series of bloodcurdling squeals, the appalling sounds of
obvious torture ceased altogether. The unsettling quiet that
followed spurred Longarm and Amos Black to feats of physical achievement typical only of men under the most severe
kinds of excessive apprehension.

The sweating, winded lawman panted to a momentary halt on the mesa near the spot where Longarm and Rebecca had earlier discovered the earless woman. "You boys went around the peak in that direction, right?" he said and pointed east with the barrel of his shotgun.

Amos nodded. "Yeah. Ain't really all that far from the cave now, Marshal. Quarter, half a mile or so at the most, I'd venture to guess. It's right at the end of a deep gully that runs almost straight east outta the base of this ugly, crumblin' chunk of fuckin' rock. Openin' ain't very big. Hard to find 'less you know where to look."

Longarm swung the shotgun around and motioned Amos ahead. "Well then, Amos," he said, "figure it's best you lead the way."

Shoulders slumped like a man being led up the last few steps of Judge Isaac Parker's Gates of Hell Gallows in Fort Smith, Black trudged past Longarm and headed into the rapidly brightening glow of a glorious, oncoming morning. He led them on a crooked, torturous route over several mesquite-and-rock-strewn hillocks. Past boulders uprooted by floods millions of years ago, then deposited in places they didn't belong. And finally, along the bottom of an extensive, narrow rift in the earth's hoary hide that abruptly ended with the pitch-black entrance to Simon Grimm's lair.

Amos Black hung back, then suddenly stepped off the trail and hid himself behind the twisted remains of a fossilized juniper bush attached to a craggy rock formation the size of a Concord coach. "Thought I could do the deed, Long. Had myself convinced I'd just hump up, bull my way right in there, kill the sonofabitch, and we'd be on our way back to Wild Horse Mesa."

Custis Long stood in the middle of the pathway leading to the cave. "Whaddya talkin' about, Amos?"

Black shook like a man in the throes of an attack of

malaria. He stared at his feet and wouldn't look Longarm in the eye. "Cain't do it, Long. Cain't go back in there. Gonna have to tackle this 'un by yourself, I guess. Ask me to do anything else for you and I'll do it. Walk into a wall of blisterin' gunfire. Hey, I'm your man. Fight off fifty screamin' bloodthirsty murderers in a half-assed fair fight, I'm your man. And hell, I'll wait right here and kill the dog shit outta Grimm first time he sticks so much as his nose outside. But don't ask me to go back into that cave. Not after what happened to me just a few hours ago. Just don't bother to ask."

Longarm stared at Black like the man had completely lost his mind. In a state of resigned acceptance, Longarm let his gaze wander around the cave entrance and then back up the trail to where Amos stood. "Alright," he said. "I'll go it alone. Flush Grimm out here to you. That work for you?"

Amos's head bobbed up and down. "Yeah. You get him out here in the open, promise I'll end his time on this earth sure as shootin'."

With no further comment, Longarm turned and marched to the dark opening in the earth. A few feet from the cave's ragged entrance, he hesitated for several seconds, then cocked the shotgun and darted inside. True to what Amos had said of the tunnel, it was darker than a pile of black cats on a moonless night. It smelled of bloody death, and every stumbling step seemed to fall on the crunching remains of piled bones.

Twenty feet or so into the cavern, a hesitant Longarm drew to a stop and held his hand up against the end of his nose. He couldn't see it. Nothing. Fingers, hand, nothing. After an uncountable number of blind, staggering steps, a soft glow deeper in the earth gradually appeared in front of him.

Using his best Comanche tiptoe, Longarm continued to creep along the fissure's damp, crumbling wall. But then, a few steps away from the source of the feeble illumination, he came to a sudden halt. A series of weirdly peculiar, unidentifiable sounds from outside swept up from behind him like an invisible wave. Can't imagine what in the hell Amos is doing out there, the puzzled lawman thought.

"Man might've been closer to snappin' his twig than I'd imagined," he whispered to himself, then headed toward the light again.

Of a sudden, the narrow dirt-and-rock passageway took a ninety degree turn to the right. To his astonishment, it opened up on a grand, vaulted, stone grotto. As Longarm gazed into the cavern in amazement, there was a curious rushing sound and fluttering movement behind him, like bats on the wing. Then the world suddenly went sideways. A strange, swirling pool of black water filled with shooting stars opened at his feet. He dove into the vaguely familiar pond like an old prospector searching for gold on the silt-covered bed of a bottomless river. 'Round and 'round he whirled, until the world faded into deep purple unconsciousness, and the eddying, ebony waters engulfed him.

For some reason, a spot deep inside Longarm's brain itched like crazy. He kept trying to scratch the irritating site, but his fingers had somehow turned into huge, strange sausages. He couldn't even get the smallest of them inserted into his ear. Then weird cackling laughter sliced through the blackest part of oblivion and jerked him back to reality.

Longarm's aching head lolled from one shoulder to the other. He tried to raise his chin off his chest. With the return of something akin to reasoned thought, he wondered how long he'd been out. After what seemed like hours of concentrated effort, he finally got his head high enough to get a look at where he'd landed.

Fifteen or twenty feet across the stone room, the barely conscious deputy marshal spotted the comatose figure of Amos Black. His friend appeared to be hog-tied to a rudely crafted cross made from the salvaged limbs of wind-blasted mesquite trees. A strange, near-naked, demonic figure painted with swatches of black and earthen-colored hues danced about in front of Longarm's insensible friend. Stringy braids swirled around the bizarre dancer's head as he whooped, chattered, giggled, jabbered nonsense, cavorted, and made bizarre gestures at the big man's unmoving figure with a huge double-edged ax.

"Gotcha, gotcha, gotcha. Snick, snick, snickety, snick. Rubadub, rubadub, rubadub. Higglety pigglety. Higglety pigglety. Higglety pigglety," the dancing figure burbled like some kind of crazed child.

"Shit," Longarm snarled under his breath. "How long have I been out?" Then, as if to an invisible friend, he muttered, "Grimm's gone completely 'round the bend. If brain cells were twigs for a fire, the crazy sonofabitch wouldn't have two of 'em left to rub against each other. Guess I'd best get my shit lined up and put an end to this lunacy."

He reached for the Frontier model Colt pistol that usually rested in the cross-draw holster at his left hip. To his eternal surprise, the astonished lawman discovered that he, too, was lashed upon a crude wooden cross—his hands and feet tightly bound with thin strips of chewed rawhide.

"Holy shit," Longarm yelped and jerked benumbed arms against the snugly tied, blood-stopping bonds.

Across the room, Simon Grimm turned into stone. He ceased dancing and became a human statue rooted to a dusty spot a few feet in front of the insensible Amos Black.

As if on some kind of metal mechanism, Grimm's head ratcheted Longarm's direction on its narrow, bony stalk. When his wild-eyed, not-of-this-life gaze finally lighted on the struggling deputy U.S. marshal, he set to whooping again, then hopped across the room like a gargantuan, crazed West Texas jackrabbit.

"Hoobajooba. Hoobajooba. Hoobajooba," the wild man chanted with each stuttering hop until he drew to a weaving stop barely a foot away from Longarm's now inert, amazed figure. "Gotcha, gotcha, gotcha," Grimm snorted, then swung the glistening ax. Its finely honed blade whistled to within an inch of the astonished lawdog's nose.

"Take your head off. Take your head off. Anytime. Anytime," Grimm chanted and flashed a maniac's grin.

Longarm gave a muscle-knotting pull at his restraints. The dried leather strips wrapped around his right wrist stretched and creaked. The tree branch he was strapped against made a barely detectable cracking noise. He snatched a glance at his hand hoping to find a weakened spot in the leather bindings or the tree limb. To his dumbfounded horror, not five feet from the tips of his fingers hung the butchered remnants of what had been another man. Good God, he thought, I recognize the pants and boots. It's Petey Baxter. Christ, where's his head?

Longarm heaved and bucked, but couldn't free himself. His seemingly futile struggles set Simon Grimm off into a fit of insane, skin-prickling laughter. The demon of Palo Duro set the head of his ax on the dirt floor. Then he did a jig around the handle. "Cain't get loose. Cain't get loose," he said. "Gonna eatcha. Gonna eatcha. Gonna eatcha."

Longarm's eyes bugged out with the strain of violent exertion. "You come close to me, you crazy bastard," he yelled, "and I'll rip your heart out and jam it up your idiotic ass."

Grimm suddenly stopped his lunatic dance. He waggled

a finger at the struggling lawman. "No, you won't," he said. "No, you won't. You can't. Stuck, you are. Stuck till you're dead. Then I'll eatcha, eatcha, eatcha."

Longarm glared at Grimm. "You're crazier'n a mattress fulla bedbugs, you loony sack of shit."

Grimm tossed his head back, giggled, and then slapped one leg as though he'd just heard a funny joke. The greasy, mud-caked, waist-length braids swished from side to side against his back. He grabbed the ax handle and flipped the deadly tool onto his shoulder. "Gonna chop you into a buncha tiny little pieces. Fry you up in my fryin' pan." He flicked an oddly colored tongue across cracked lips. "Lickety good. Lickety good. Lickety good."

Longarm pulled at his bonds again, then slumped against the tree. "Kiss my ass, you crazy bastard," he yelled.

Grimm took a surprised step backward. Crazed eyes danced in his painted face like the flames of hell. "Maybe, I'll wait. Maybe, I'll wait. Yep. Yep. Yep. Too stringy. Too stringy. Tall, lean, and stringy. Your friend'll be tastier. Bigger, meatier."

In a fit of madcap lunacy, Grimm pranced back across the room, past a smoldering fire of sticks, limbs, and twigs. A bubbling, blackened pot hung over the fire from an iron spit. The odor that wafted off the cooking contents and swirled up Longarm's nose came nigh on to inducing a state of uncontrollable nausea.

Grimm drew to a stop near Amos Black's motionless form again, then raised the ax with one hand and ran a thumb along its glistening, well-honed edge. "Sharp. Sharp, it is. Take his head off. Take his head off. Yes. Yes. Yes."

As Grimm brought the blade up and back, Longarm twisted back and forth. Yelled, "No, don't do it, you crazy bastard."

Grimm glanced over his shoulder at his struggling captive

and flashed a maniacal grin. He rubbed his dripping nose against a naked shoulder, then said, "This here big ole boy's got some fine-lookin' haunches. Gonna be mighty fine eatin'. Yessir. Mighty fine eatin'. Taste like chicken. Taste like chicken."

The lunatic swiveled his fractured attention back to Amos Black. He brought the ax's handle up and rested it on his right shoulder in the classic wood-chopping pose. Resettled his grip on the tool's hickory handle and raised it above his head. "Snick, snick, snickety, snick," he chanted.

Longarm turned his head away from the action. But then, tightly closed eyes snapped open when he heard, "Drop that ax, you crazy son of a bitch. Step away from him and drop that ax."

Grimm's mad-eyed gaze swung to the grotto's entry. Longarm followed the madman's wobbling gape. In gasping breaths, he offered up silent thanks to God and watched the stringy-muscled figure of Rebecca McCabe stride to the middle of the stone room, shotgun snugged firmly against her shoulder.

Grimm crouched like a cornered animal. He brought the ax up high over his head as though ready to kill the woman at the first opportunity. His eyes bugged and smoldered. Strange grunts and creepy twitterings issued from his gap-toothed mouth. He scuttled to one side like a frightened rock scorpion. He appeared on the verge of heading for the safety of the tunnel at a dead run.

Rebecca stopped a few steps from the harebrained man's flickering fire pit. "Take one more step, Grimm, and it'll be your last. I'll cut you in two, right where you stand."

Palo Duro's resident madman stopped dead in his tracks. "Dreams. Dreams. Dreams. Seen you in my dreams. Death. Death. Death. You're the death bringer, missy. Yes. Yes. Yes. The death bringer."

With Grimm still lined up behind the bead between her shotgun's barrels, Rebecca called out over one shoulder, "You alright, Long? Didn't hurt you, did he?"

Longarm gave a vigorous shake of the head. "No. No. I'm fine. Just get on over here and cut me loose, 'Becca. Don't wait. Do it now."

"What about Amos?"

"Think he's okay, just unconscious. Loco sonofabitch, Grimm, musta got behind us before we ever made it to the entrance of this fetid hidey-hole. Did a helluva number on the pair of us. Grinning idiot caught me with my pants down like a ten-year-old boy showin' his stuff off to an inquisitive sister."

Ax still poised above his grimy head, Grimm suddenly took several bold but ill-considered steps Rebecca's direction. "Snick, snick, snickety, snick. I'll put a nick in you, bitch. Snick, snick, snickety, snick," Grimm sang.

The big blaster clasped in the girl's fingers roared to life. A heavy-gauge wad of buckshot the size of a Mexican sombrero caught the ax-wielding Grimm in the leg, snatched the limb from beneath him, and knocked the squealing loon onto his belly in an explosive flash of thunderous, rolling gunpowder.

Chapter 17

Before the blue black cloud of spent gunpowder from Rebecca McCabe's shotgun had managed to dissipate, she was at Longarm's side, knife in hand, whittling at his restraints. One arm dropped free, but the astonished lawdog found the floppy appendage had grown so numb from the constriction of blood that he had trouble raising it.

"Thought I told you to stay behind with the woman," he hissed into her ear.

"She's dead, Custis. Died not long after you and Amos started hoofin' your way up here. Figured I'd sneak in and make sure you boys got the job done right."

"Well, have to admit, I'm damned sure glad to see you, girl. 'Bout as happy as a man can be." He knifed a hasty glance across the room, then said, "Christ, 'Becca, Grimm's up."

Rebecca McCabe slapped the knife into Longarm's almost useless hand, then twirled around just in time to spot Simon Grimm dragging himself their direction. Somehow, the seriously wounded fiend had employed the ax handle to pull himself upright. Now he worked the hideous weapon like a cane as he dragged a useless, shattered, blood-oozing leg across the grotto's gore-littered floor.

The double-barreled blaster snapped to Rebecca's shoulder. Another thunderous, well-placed shot sliced Grimm's remaining prop from beneath him. In a howling fit of flying flesh and a misty spray of blood, the murderer of unnumbered people went to the ground like a sackful of anvils. The ax flew from his grasp and landed several feet away. Yowling like a wounded animal, he rolled onto his back, then, to Longarm and Rebecca's stunned surprise, desperately tried to sit up.

Of a sudden, a sinister rumble surged through the entirety of Grimm's earthen hideout. Every conscious, living soul in the cavern gasped and shot worried glances toward the cave's ceiling. Loose gravel and chunks of sandstone shale broke away from the grotto's roof, thudded to the floor, and exploded in clouds of dust and splintered rock.

With buckets of rubble raining down on her shoulders, Rebecca breeched the Greener, pulled the empty brass casings out, dropped them on the ground, and expertly reloaded. Then she snatched the knife from Longarm's tingling fingers and sawed him completely free of his leather fetters.

"Best get Amos down quick as you can, Custis," she said. "Try to bring him back to sensibility. We've gotta get out of here. And from the look and sound of it, pretty damned fast like."

Longarm followed Rebecca's darting gaze as it careened to the grotto's crumbling roof.

"Think the whole mountain is about to come in on us," she added. "Touchin' this big popper off down here most certainly didn't help any. Now go get Amos loose. I'll take care of Mr. Simon Grimm."

On barely feeling legs, Longarm staggered to Amos Black's side and in short order freed the man's hands and feet. Amos slumped into a moaning heap on the cave's floor. A slap to the face brought him around. He crawled on hands and knees for nearly a minute before he was able to stand.

Black rubbed his benumbed legs and took several tentative, wobbling steps. Came nigh on to falling again, then said, "Sorry 'bout all this, Marshal Long. Sneaky sonofabitch got behind me somehow." He rubbed a spot on the back of his head. "Still don't know what he hit me with. Got a knot the size of a duck egg just behind my left ear. Really put me down, that's for damned sure."

Longarm ran fingers through his own hair, then said, "No need to apologize. Got its twin brother on my noggin. 'Pears I didn't come anywhere close to suspecting how cunning the sorry bastard was either. Yep, misjudged the sneaky skunk for sure and certain."

Both men turned when they heard Rebecca McCabe growl, "You've butchered your last human being, Grimm. Swear 'fore Jesus, you'll never hurt another livin' person."

"Oh God. Oh God. Oh God," the injured butcher cried out. "Please don't hurt Simon. Please don't hurt Simon. He's hurt enough. Legs hurt. Hurt real bad. Pain. Pain. Oh, such pain."

Longarm got Amos Black's enormous arm across his shoulders and helped the big man lumber toward the cavern's rapidly crumbling entrance. At the arched entryway, he stopped long enough to shoot a glance back Simon Grimm's direction and saw Rebecca standing over the wounded lunatic, shotgun pointed at the injured man-eater's head.

Longarm called out, "Come on, 'Becca. Way the roof's crumblin', it's gonna come down on the lot of us just about any second now. Leave him. God'll take care of it."

"No," she yelled back. "No, I won't. I'll take care of it."

"Well, then, do whatever you're gonna do and let's get the hell out." When he got no response, he yelled, "You hear me, girl? You payin' attention, or did you suddenly go deaf?"

Rebecca McCabe's piercing gaze never left Simon Grimm's knotted, cowering form. "Go on ahead," she yelled over the earth's escalating reverberations. "I'll be right behind you. Have one or two little things to take care of first. Don't worry. I won't be long."

The narrowness of the passageway to safety forced Longarm to push, pull, shove, and then damn near drag Amos Black to the outside. Along the way he wondered how Grimm had managed to drag the two of them inside. Hell of a trick, he thought.

As the duo stumbled into welcomed daylight, twin shotgun blasts echoed along the dark corridor behind them and brought both men up short. Then a hair-raising roar growled its way from deep inside Simon Grimm's hideout. The thunderous rumble washed over them in a wave of roiling dust and debris that spurted from the cave's entrance as though squeezed through a blacksmith's bellows.

Enveloped in a fast-moving, reddish brown cloud, Longarm stood his ground and coughed. He snatched his hat off, waved as much of the flying grit away from his face as possible, and waited for the grimy, curtainlike veil of grit to pass. Just when he feared he might never see Rebecca McCabe again, the astonishing woman strolled through the powdery haze like a woman on her way to Sunday school. Chin up and jaw clenched, she stopped a few feet away.

"You okay?" Longarm said.

"Yeah," Amos Black sputtered, "you okay, Rebecca? That sonofabitch hurt you?"

"Just fine as frog hair." She breeched the shotgun. Discarded another set of spent casings, reloaded, and snapped the gun closed with dripping, blood-saturated fingers. She propped the weapon's stock against one hip, then said,

"Won't have to worry 'bout Simon Grimm anymore, boys. Fact is no one else in the whole world will ever have to worry 'bout that flesh-eatin' skunk—God as my witness."

"What'd you do, Rebecca?" Longarm said.

She laid the big popper's barrel across her shoulders, draped one arm over the stock, the other over the barrel. Then she pushed several steps past her dust-covered companions. Stopped and turned on her heel to face them again. "What'd I tell you I was gonna do, Marshal Long? You remember? Made my intentions about as clear as a barrel of fresh rainwater from the very beginning."

Longarm ran several fingers under his hat band and scratched a spot over one ear. He toed at the dirt, then shot a horrified look at the woman and said, "Aw, jeeze, 'Becca. You didn't. Tell me you didn't actually do that."

"What? What'd she tell you, Long?" Amos said. "Come on, let it out. Shouldn't keep stuff from me, you know."

A sad, sardonic smile tinged Rebecca McCabe's lips when she said, "Swore it on the graves of my dead family, Long. No way out of a promise made before God and the dead. For longer'n I care to think on, my whole world's been tilted askew because of insane acts committed by Simon Grimm. Well, everything's a bit better now. World's *almost* upright again. Comin' 'round to damn near shipshape. Only thing left for me to do is to somehow make my way back to the Green River country. Visit those graves one more time, and tell the gnawed-on remains of those butchered folks they can rest easy."

"What? What'd she do?" Amos groaned.

Rebecca flipped the shotgun up and rested the stock against one hip. "Placed the muzzle of my father's smoke pole against that murderin' bastard's chest and blew his heart out his back. Used my bowie on 'im. Severed the totality of his manhood and stuffed it all in his mouth. Unfortunately, I didn't have time enough to set his sorry ass on fire. But, as luck would have it, God took care of buryin' what was left of 'im for me." Then she turned on her heel and left both men staring at her in disbelief.

Longarm shook his head in dumbfounded incredulity. He motioned for Amos Black to follow. They fell in behind Rebecca as she picked her way back down the draw, then headed for the river and Goodnight's dugout. They'd gone but a few steps when Longarm grinned and said, "You're a hard case, woman. Real flinty piece of work, if I've ever seen one. Yessir, I've known some hard cases in my time, but, by God, I do believe you'd take the cake if we were givin' out prizes."

Amos Black could do little but stumble along and shake his head. "Took his manhood, huh?" he muttered.

Over her shoulder Rebecca called, "You two stop usin' up brain space thinkin' 'bout me. We've still got what's left of a poor, sad woman in camp to bury."

Billy Vail pushed himself back in his overstuffed office chair, then jerked the smoldering cigar from between stammering lips. "S-s-swear 'fore the Good Lord, Custis, you've come in here and told some amazin' tales, but this 'un has to go d-d-down as the absolute nickel-plated, top rung on the ladder."

Longarm thumped an inch-long chunk of burned tobacco off his five-cent cheroot. A mass of ash dropped into his boss's strange, apple-shaped, glass ashtray balanced on one of Longarm's legs. "Well, it's all the God's truth, Billy. Wanna check out my report there. Story makes for a helluva good read. Swear it ain't no windy whizzer either. Didn't have to make a single word of that stuff up."

"Simon Grimm truly was a cannibal? You have no doubt as to the validity of such an accusation?"

"Hell, no. Not from what I saw in that snake pit of a cave

where he was livin', down in Palo Duro Canyon. Bodies and parts of bodies everywhere you could lay an eye. You add that to what Marshal Talbot Butterworth in Mesquite told me 'bout what the crazy bastard did to the corpses of our friends George Brackett and Junior Pelts. Then you factor in the insanity Rebecca McCabe related to me of what actually happened over in the Green River country, and well, I just don't see how you can come to any other conclusion."

Vail puffed at his stogie. For some seconds he said nothing. Then he scratched his near-hairless pate with one finger. "Amos make it back home alright?"

"Yeah. Said he might not ever leave that collection of oddities again. Told me he'd had about all of people he could use for some years to come. Man sure as hell wouldn't be goin' out on any more expeditions with me, even if I am a friend of yours."

Vail nodded, then pointed with his cigar at Longarm and said, "Glad to hear Amos is okay. No doubt, you're absolutely right about Grimm. But, look, I'd appreciate it if you wouldn't spread any of this around just yet. Word will eventually get back to Amarillo and Mesquite if you do. No point sending folks into a panic since the danger's already passed. Let a yarn about cannibals get goin' good, and there's just no telling how it'll all come to an end. 'Fore you know it, we'll have people eaters poppin' out from behind every rock between Denver and Phoenix and from there back to Fort Smith."

Longarm stuffed his hat on. He clambered from the leather-covered guest chair, placed the odd, apple-shaped ashtray back on Vail's desk, then straightened his suit jacket and resettled his pistol belt. "Well, whatever you want just suits me right down to the ground, Billy. Won't say a word 'bout people eatin' each other to anyone in Denver. Leastways, not until you tell me it's okay."

As the lanky deputy U.S. marshal reached for the knob on the office door, Billy Vail called out, "Anything in this report of yours that explains why it took you a week longer than it should have to get back to Denver, Custis?"

A wickedly impish grin had etched its way onto Custis Long's lips when he turned and said, "Well, as a matter of pure fact, boss, the lovely Rebecca McCabe and me decided to see the sights around Mesquite and Amarillo. Tour took us a bit longer than I originally expected."

Marshal Vail's brows knotted. He scratched his belly, took a puff off his cigar, then said, "What the hell sights are you talkin' about, Custis? What tour? Ain't no sights to see anywhere close to Amarillo, 'cept maybe Palo Duro Canyon. Hell, you'd just come from there."

Longarm threw his head back and laughed, then said, "Think about it, Billy. Come on, think about it."

Vail could still hear Longarm cackling as the stalwart deputy marshal hit the staircase at the end of the hall. The grinning chief U.S. marshal took a puff from his cigar, then smiled and to the banjo clock on his wall said, "The woman, of course. Bet neither one of 'em ever got outta bed the whole week. That's Longarm alright. Shoulda known. Just shoulda known."

Watch for

**LONGARM AND THE
MISSING BRIDE**

the 364th novel in the exciting LONGARM
series from Jove

Coming in March!